The TAF Omnibus Vol. III

Triangle Association of Freelancers

(Stories, Essays & Poems)

Arlene S. Bice, Editor

For information about TAF and the authors published within, visit the TAF website at www.tafnc.com.

Cover Design by: humblenations@gmail.com
James@GoOnWrite.com

Project Editor: Arlene S. Bice

Dedication

This book is dedicated to all writers
both novice and professional
to keep writings by human beings prominent.
May one help another through encouragement
and kindness.

Additional TAF Publications

A Taste of Taffy: Samplings from TAF
TAF Stays Home: 29 Freelancers Writing
The TAF Reader: Books on a Freelance Writer's Shelf
The TAF Omnibus: Stories & Poems
The TAF Omnibus Vol. II (Stories, Essays, & Poems)

*What an astonishing thing a book is.
It's a flat object made from a tree with
flexible parts on which are imprinted
lots of funny dark squiggles. But one
glance at it and you're inside the mind
of another person ...*
Carl Sagan

A Brief History of TAF

Triangle Association of Freelancers (TAF) is unique among writing organizations in that it is, at heart, a family. Our members applaud each other's successes and commiserate over our disappointments. We share information about markets and job opportunities, and mentor those who are new to the profession. Because of this sincere familial support, TAF has grown and flourished.

TAF was established in 2003 and became a nonprofit in 2017. We held our first conference in 2008, and another each year after, until forced to take a temporary hiatus in 2020 because of the COVID pandemic. In lieu of an in-person event, we quickly pivoted to a series of moderated online conversations with prominent writers, editors, and other industry professionals that we call TAF Talks. Indeed, through the years, TAF has proved itself to be the Little Writing Community That Could. While staying true to our Tarheel roots, we have expanded our reach to surrounding states and even across the country, offering support, networking, advice, and mentoring to writers in all forms and genres. In numerous instances, membership in TAF has led to a writer's first publication.

This book is another example of TAF's growing voice within the broader writing community. Technically our sixth group anthology, it is both a fundraiser for the organization and a showcase for our members' works. For some, this is their first publication.

Triangle Association of Freelancers is a family, one with broad, outstretched arms. We're always eager to meet new writers, discuss what they're working on, and see how we can help them achieve their goals. Our members are multi-published, and award-winning. If you are not already a member, I encourage you to learn more about who we are and what we have to offer by visiting our website: https://tafnc.com.

In the meantime, enjoy the stories, essays, and poems offered for this anthology. They come from the heart, and hopefully will inspire you to put your own stories on paper.

--Don Vaughan, Founder
Triangle Association of Freelancers
Raleigh, NC

Introduction

The Best Time to Write Is…
Now is the best time to write, even in a time filled with new technology (such as Artificial Intelligence apps), distractions, and other challenges.

Why? Because the writers who came before us also wrote during times when new inventions, interruptions, life's challenges, and other changes surrounded them.

The need for writers to share their stories remains unchanged. A story that needs to be shared lies within us, even when we are completely silent.

Maya Angelou (previously named Marguerite Annie Johnson as a child) was quiet for a few years, after a traumatic experience during her childhood. Little Marguerite then met a woman named Bertha Flowers, who lived in Marguerite's community.

In her autobiography, I Know Why the Caged Bird Sings, Maya Angelou writes about her childhood trauma, her decision to stop talking, and about Ms. Flowers sharing books with her. Ms. Flowers sharing her knowledge helped Maya rediscover her own voice and grow up to become a famous poet, author, and multi-talented creative professional.

The need to write and share stories is a major source of inspiration for the TAF Omnibus: Stories, Essays & Poems Vol. III. This latest edition of the TAF Omnibus is an important contribution to Triangle Association of Freelancers' history, which spans more than 20 years.

During this time, our organization has grown into one of the largest writing organizations in North Carolina. TAF's mission is to provide networking, education, and mentoring to writers in all genres. We're proud to have inspired and helped many writers start (or restart) their writing careers, publish their first books, and find other ways to succeed with other types of writing opportunities.

The TAF Omnibus is a fundraiser for the organization, but more importantly, it's an opportunity to share and feature our members' writings.

We hope you enjoy the stories, poems, essays and more within this book. May they inspire you to create, write and share your own stories.

- *Maya Spikes*, Executive Director
Triangle Association of Freelancers

Table of Contents

5	A Brief History of TAF	
7	Introduction	
11	Forget Me Not	Lavoie-Vaughan
18	Buried	Ryan
19	Responsibility	Ryan
20	A Day at the Beach	Badger
31	Feathered Travel Time	Badger
32	In search of 'telligent life	Rumble
36	It was nature	Rumble
37	Take the Power Back	Wizenberg
52	Fly, Baby, Fly	LaMotta
57	Autumn's Debut	LaMotta
58	My Moment in Time	LaMotta
59	The Blank Page	LaMotta
61	Blessed and Highly Favored	Henderson-Daye
68	Moments of Dis-Grace	Brookshire
70	Harry the Frog	Clemmons
80	The Visitor	Bartholomew
81	First Chapter	McCorvey
88	God is The Author	Brennan
93	The Time Stamp	Brennan
98	Beautiful Teeth	Hoffman
103	Know But to God	Michels
106	Ode to a Sea Creature	Toman
108	Margaritaville	Toman
112	Chapter 6 from Obscura	Harmon
123	Cardinal Dreams	Tomey-Zonneveld

Table of Contents.... Continued

124   Love Knots   Tomey-Zonneveld
125   Band on the Run, Again   Tomey-Zonneveld
125   Freedom Flight   Tomey-Zonneveld
125   a space above my head   Tomey-Zonneveld
126   World's Greatest Burger   Vaughan
137   He'd Survived Vietnam   Pennington
144   The Count   Pennington
145   The Ivory Silk Peignoir Set   Bice

155   About Our Authors
160   About the Editor
161   Acknowledgements
162   Membership

Nanette Lavoie-Vaughan is an advanced practice nurse who has published clinical articles and book chapters and is the author of Healing Energy, Healing Hands, a guide to Therapeutic Touch. This is her first published short story.

Forget Me Not

Emma stared at the flat silver pronged object in front of her and concentrated. The synapses in the memory storage area of her brain crackled and sparked furiously attempting to retrieve data. Any clue that might help her to remember the purpose of the object or the name. Nothing was found and the electrical activity began to slow.

A young black woman in a rumpled blue uniform sat directly in front of Emma. She kept placing the object in Emma's gnarled hand and giving her a command: "Eat". The object was covered with a lump of white, soft material. Emma continued to stare blankly, no visible sign of recognition on her wrinkled face or in her cloudy brown eyes.

Emma was sitting in the day room, absently running her hands across the surface of the tray in front of her. She was positioned in a geriatric chair, a large highchair-like device that restrained confused adults, in view of the television to provide auditory and visual stimulation while the staff started their preparations for evening baths and bedtime.

Her mind began to ruminate. Fuzzy images of the man she had been conversing with daily for the last year surfaced and Emma's intuition sensed that he played an important role in her present position. The visits had become a comfortable part of Emma's daily routine. The companionship and social interaction had been enthusiastically received by Emma who had been increasingly isolated after her husband's death two years ago. Although she had been considered an independent woman by her contemporaries; Murray's death had affected her more greatly than anyone would ever know.

They shared an ideal relationship for forty-eight years, being friends, lovers and partners. They had raised their daughter with the values that molded their relationship.

Emma always worked outside the home and shared the household responsibilities with Murray, balancing both with equal aplomb even before women's liberation was a whisper. But it was exactly that type of life that made it impossible for Emma to exist without Murray.

Theirs was a symbiotic relationship and with one partner gone, the vitality, the need and the drive to go on was absent. It was Murray who provided the spark for Emma to be the career minded housewife of her generation. Without his daily presence and with her daughter grown and settled in her own career, life no longer served a purpose.

Emma began to withdraw into herself, severing the ties she had with friends and relegated herself to going through the motions of everyday life. Eating when the mood struck her, reading the accumulation of books and magazines and her weekly bridge games. So, when the man appeared in her living room that first evening the spark began to crackle and burn.

Emma could not remember all the details of their meetings, but she knew that it had been wonderful to have someone to talk to, who wanted to hear everything about her and the many facets of her life. Every evening, she would recant another episode of her life. She started with her most recent as they were the most precious memories and helped to keep alive Murray's presence in her life.

Gradually she began to go further and further back. The man was a skilled listener and Emma felt a sense of peace and calm after each visit. By the time Emma realized that those shared memories had disappeared, never to be retrieved again, it was too late. That's when the strangers had entered and tried to help her. Intuitively, Emma knew that she needed assistance because even daily tasks were becoming too complex.

She had just told the man about a wonderful holiday feast she had prepared for the family and now she couldn't even prepare morning tea. Maybe she was just overtired from the late-night talks. She would let them help her temporarily until this annoying memory loss passed as she was one who had never lost at anything she set out to do. She resolved to get more sleep and keep up her strength.

Emma had been a resident of the Lake Crystal Nursing Center Alzheimer's Unit for a month. She had been placed there by her daughter when it became distressingly apparent that it was unsafe for her to remain in her retirement condo. A string of embarrassing incidents with her neighbors involving stolen laundry, to midnight visits and voiced concerns from Emma's bridge partners had forced Pearl to contact Emma's physician for advice.

He reassured her that memory loss was a common phenomenon in the elderly and that he would prescribe a medication that increased circulation in the brain which had been known to be helpful in these circumstances. As an afterthought, he also mentioned a home health agency to check in on her periodically.

Several days later, Pearl received a phone call from Ann Burns, the nursing supervisor at Professional Nursing Inc., who informed her that her staff had evaluated her mother's situation, and they would be providing her mother a home health aide for personal care and shopping, a nurse to monitor her response to her medication and a social worker to assist with transportation and housekeeping needs. Not a thing to worry about, all was covered by her mother's Medicare and if a problem arose, they would call. Pearl's anxiety level decreased perceptibly; the problem was solved. Until the call came about a month later.

Waves of anxiety mixed with dread rolled across Pearl's consciousness as she reached for the phone. Mrs. Burns was polite but blunt, Pearl needed to come to Florida as soon as possible to make alternative arrangements for her mother. She highlighted the most recent concerns reported by her staff: a gas burner left on overnight, meandering aimlessly in the parking lot, and conversations with a strange man who appeared in her living room each evening. Maybe it would be best if she was placed in a nursing home with twenty-four-hour supervision. After several hurried phone calls and a frenzy of packing, Pearl was on a red-eye flight to south Florida.

Upon her arrival at Emma's condo, Pearl was dismayed at the degree of deterioration her mother displayed. Although she appeared to recognize Pearl, her eyes exhibited a dull luster that mirrored the thought processes necessary to remember and identify her daughter. Her clothing hung about her rail-thin body like sack cloth. She was now a meek, mumbling shadow of the once vital and active woman that Pearl had tried to emulate in her adulthood.

Any attempt at conversation was futile; Pearl only had two verbal tapes that her mind allowed her to play repeatedly. The first was a reminiscent tale of how as a young woman she had worked at the first area hospital and the responsibilities which the position entailed, which changed slightly with each telling of the tale. The second was merely a statement of how she had a lovely conversation with the man in her living room.

The nursing assistant tried several more attempts to get Emma to eat but was unable to get her to focus. She reluctantly removed the food tray and began the preparations to get Emma settled in bed for the night. A quick sponge bath and a fresh gown completed her routine and Emma was back in bed with the lights dimmed. Emma lay still looking at the shadows in the room. Suddenly a familiar voice startled her. She saw the familiar mam standing at the end of her bed.

"It is time Emma", he whispered. "You have served my purpose, and I shall now bring you peace." "My name is Jordan, and I needed your memories to save my wife. I come from a future where we have discovered how to restore a person's memory by matching them with someone from the past. In your time, the removal of your memories was called dementia. No one suspected it was my people stealing your memories." Jordan moved closer to the bed and placed his hand on Emma's chest and emitted a pulse of energy into her heart, stopping her heartbeat.

A nursing assistant was passing by Emma's room and thought she heard an unfamiliar voice. This was not the first time this had happened on the night shift. She stepped into the room and thought she saw a shadow in the corner near Emma's bed but passed it off as a trick of light from the nearby window. She approached the bed and noticed that Emma was smiling and was not breathing. She checked for a pulse and found none. Leaving the room to notify the nurse, she puzzled over how it seemed that there was more unexplained whispering and deaths at night. But she passed it off as a normal part of working in a dementia unit.

Jordan leaned over the woman lying in peaceful repose on the gurney. His hand brushed across her brow gently rearranging the wisp of hair curled there. The procedure had successfully taken place this morning and the wait would soon be over. Helena, his partner and life mate, would return to him with her memory restored. The medical team assured him that their extensive research had identified the cause of Helena's problem, and the simple operation would reverse all effects the condition had on her brain. The months of uncertainty and the concerns of a bleak future were now erased by the prospects of success.

Nanette Lavoie-Vaughan

Sarah Merritt Ryan is a poet, blogger, and writer of memoir. She writes of her experiences with emotionally surviving serious mental illness, expressing her unique story. Her poetry has been published by Whispering Angels Books, Prolific Pulse Press, PurpleStone Press, Garden of Neuro Institute, and Fine Lines Literary Journal.

Buried

Moonlight shines as bold and bright sky anew
Never find I peace from seeking daylight
Find trouble when I open my eyes true
Truth entangles with burden in hindsight.

My survival a sure relic of gold
My will to live proof of what's worth struggle
Pushing hard for my story to be told
Challenging untold pains I can juggle.

Uncovered tales ache and burn deep inside
Release them all flying high and away
Hurt first letting go but quickly subside
Catharsis a new creation to stay.

Doubleminded willingness to disclose
Persistent work in time believes it knows.

Responsibility

Time falls away as I exit my prime
Silence inside echoes and prods me through
Sands slip through fingers my passage of time
Life is my teacher, a starkness that's true.

Love and loss, victories both uncover
Joy and suffering, the greatest of stakes
Myself, burden and gift to another
Mistakes and learning what true success makes.

Suffering I thought was long gone and past
Fears of unveiling a divergent path
Collecting strength to persevere at last
Shutting down unimaginable wrath.

One slippery slope of stability
My mind a tough responsibility.

Sarah Merritt Ryan

Nancy Lee Badger grew up on New York's Long Island. She swam at beaches on both the north and south shores. After marrying her college sweetheart and raising two sons in New Hampshire, Nancy moved to North Carolina. She's published in romance, a blogger, reviewer, and member of the Triangle Association of Freelancers.

A Day at the Beach

The moment I turned off the ignition and opened my car door, the brilliant afternoon sun blinded me. Squinting, I slammed the door shut behind me. Opening the rear passenger door by feel, I grabbed my plaid beach bag.

"How could I forget my sunglasses? Unforgivable."

A curse slipped out, then I took in a long, slow breath. Why hadn't I written a list before heading to the sandy shores of Kill Devil Hills? Memories of the stinging words that co-workers back in New York City had branded me still hurt. *You are such a silly list maker!*" They could be right, due to the way I organized my old life. Moving to Elizabeth City in the 'sunny south' had been a spur of the moment decision. My determination to make a life in eastern North Carolina starts with a dip in the ocean.

It's only May. Memorial Day is around the corner. Before moving down, I'd heard the water warmed quickly in North Carolina. Back home, my former home, the water is barely above freezing. Unfortunately for my fair skin and blue eyes, the sun reigned.

Turning over a car blanket and snow brush, both no longer needed in the sunny south, I fished out an old baseball cap. It's an ugly purple color sporting a football team logo and had belonged to my ex.

"It will have to do."

Heading toward the wooden walkway that led up and over the dunes, I stopped at the apex. Feathery sea oats and the woody branches of seashore elders fluttered in the breeze beside me. The glare coming off the wide expanse of ocean blinded me again. Snapping my eyes shut, my hand shot out and clutched the handrail.

In a combination of shock at the brightness and exuberance due to my love of the water, I skipped blindly down the wooden walkway toward the sand. Opening my eyes into tiny slits, the sight of a surfer cresting a large foaming wave caught my attention and I hurried to find a spot on the beach.

A footstep later I tripped over something hard. Flying forward, I tumbled facedown into the sand while my belongings flew elsewhere.

"I beg yer pardon, lass," bellowed a deep voice. The sound, more like gravel than human, with apparent anger fueling his words made me gasp. Before I could think of a response, he added, "Forgive me for sunbathing where ye chanced to walk."

"Dear Lord!" Jumping up with both arms wind milling for purchase, I tried to regain my footing. My knees shook and I fell backward. As I sucked in a breath to scream, the scent of coconut oil and salty air teased my nose.

About to land on my rear end, a large palm with meaty fingers latched onto my arm and drew me to my feet. Once steady, the mystery hand disappeared. A shadow replaced the sun, so I glanced up.

Way, way up.

Swallowing partly from fear and mostly from embarrassment, I blinked. How could I have been so blind? I might have hurt someone. Stepping back a foot or two, I narrowed my eyes. That damn sun is back!
I blinked and a thought struck me, making me throw a hand up to block the rays. I fully opened my eyes. "Where's my hat?"

Ignoring the mountain of a man in front of me, I swung toward the water and searched for the hat that had flown off my head, along with the missing beach bag. The bag lay a few yards away. I rushed over, grabbed it, and made sure my cell phone hadn't slipped out.

"Praise the Lord!" I found it still inside and not buried in the sand. But where is my cap?

"Be ye looking for this, lass?"

A shiver snaked its way up my spine, making both shoulders quake. The voice with the sexy accent must be right behind me. What had he asked? I turned to face him and spied the baseball cap in his hand.

"Ye like this sport? I myself enjoy a good football match, but I fear it differs from what Americans play," he said as he stared at the logo sitting above the cap's rim.

"Never mind. I forgot my sunglasses. Beggars can't be choosers, or so the saying goes, right?" I opened my palm and waited as he passed the cap to me. He began to move away, then hesitated.

"Have ye nothing to say to me?" He spoke so low his question was barely audible.

My cheeks warmed with embarrassment the moment I realized what he meant. "I am so sorry. The sun blinded me and I missed everything, including you." How I could have missed a long-legged, naked to the waist, hunk of man who… "Are you wearing a kilt?"

The colorful yellow and black pattern looked out-of-place on a beach. This brought me to my next thought.

"Do you always wear a kilt while sleeping on the sand far from the water's edge, yet close to a walkway?" Slapping the cap onto my head, I groaned as sand waterfalled onto my hair and shoulders. What a mess.

"The truth?" His dark-brown left eyebrow rose.

I laughed at the grim expression on his face. "I find truthfulness is always best. It is one of the reasons I left New York." Thinking about my unfaithful ex at the moment made me frown.

"Ah, yer a New Yorker? Well, I hail from the snowy Highlands of Scotland, hence the kilt. I wear one all the time. 'Tis comfy. Since I live far from the ocean, I never learned. To swim, I mean. I sat here and watched the men on those boards until I could not keep me eyes open. I beg yer forgiveness for foolishly sleeping over there." He pointed over his shoulder, where a beach blanket and a thermos-like bottle sat.

"You can't swim." What an insensitive comment! I learned to swim at age four at Fire Island and Sunken Meadow State Parks on Long Island. Swimming felt easy, normal, and refreshing, yet the look on this man's sun-tanned face told me he'd shared a personal truth.

"Listen. I didn't mean to state the obvious, but you really ought to learn to swim. Besides an enjoyable recreation, especially on a hot day, it could save your life."

"Are ye offering to teach me, lass?"

Gulp. "Ah, no. You ought to learn in a group or with a certified lifeguard. I only made it to Junior Lifeguard while in the Girl Scouts."

His other eyebrow rose in confusion.

"A group for young schoolgirls. It teaches them things like hiking, arts and crafts, and swimming."

He turned away and walked over to his blanket. With his back to me, I caught sight of his dark hair brushing the tanned skin at his shoulders. He turned back toward the beach and sat cross-legged. The hem of a pair of tan shorts peeked from beneath the fluttering wool. He picked up the bottle, unscrewed the lid, raised it to his lips, and drank.

I couldn't move. In the midst of an erotic scene, I thought I might melt. Then, he winked at me and took another sip.

I again watched his throat move as he swallowed, then realized my feet had brought me closer. Why? I should ignore him and head toward the water. A nice swim might be the catalyst that makes me forget the entire encounter.

He won't follow me, that's for sure. The thought made me a little sad. Why? Then the deeper questions started. Who exactly is he and why had he appeared on the exact beach I had discovered near my new home? "You don't find many hunks sporting Scottish accents and wearing kilts around Kill Devil Hills," I muttered.

"Sure you do."

I spun to my left and nearly fell on my face a second time. I took a moment to look at my new female acquaintance. My pulse slowed as I concentrated on her heart-shaped face, freckles, dark red hair tied into a pony tail…

"Careful! Wouldn't want those surfer boys to see a clumsy you."

"Thanks for pointing that out," I spat. "And, you are?"

"Penny Stewart. I hail from Elizabeth City, back over the Wright Memorial Bridge."

"Well, nice to meet you." Seeing I was close to the water's edge, I tugged my beach towel out of my tote and tossed it near her, and smiled. "I'm Reagan Brownell. I recently moved there, too."

I hadn't made many friends since moving and this girl named Penny seemed to know more about why a man with a sexy Scottish accent sat on a beach in Kill Devil Hills. Kneeling, I spread out my towel as a blanket and sat.

"Penny, please explain why I ought to know why a man like the one I just met should be sitting on this beach?"

"Scottish Highland Games," Penny said.

My mind went blank. Highland Games in North Carolina? I had heard of them, of course, since mom said we are of Scottish descent, but I'd never attended one.

"Some kind of fair or festival?" I asked.

"It's much more than that. It's a place for all people who want to celebrate their Celtic heritage to spend the day eating Scottish food, wearing kilts," Penny said as she gestured toward the hunk, "or taking part in dancing or bagpipe playing. That man signed up yesterday to compete in various athletic events. I know because my dad is one of the organizers and I helped check-in the athletes and bands."

"Bands?" I pictured young kids playing flutes or violins.

"Rock bands in kilts! Playing bagpipes and electric guitars! We have two well-known groups giving concerts throughout the day. You ought to come. Starts tomorrow." I said nothing and released a long, cleansing breath. I turned my attention to the surfers. The sun had lowered behind us, so I tossed off my cap and stood. "Excuse me, but the ocean is calling."

"Have fun. The water's fine. Maybe your new friend will join you." Penny's cheeks pinked and she covered her giggle with her hand.

I shook my head while giving her a quick smile, then walked to the water's edge. Dipping my toes into the next small wave, the coolness of the water joined the feel of the sand oozing up between my toes. I missed this. Simple, mind-easing bliss.

As I contemplated how far I should swim from shore, a shadow painted the surface. From beside me, the shadow spoke.

"Ye said ye willno' teach me, but could ye show me what 'tis so special about the sea?"

I glanced below his waist. He'd removed the kilt.

"Shorts? No swimsuit?"

"I doona' swim, so…"

"Well, they're fine. You can start with walking beside me in the shallows. I'm happy to wade along the shore with you."

His smile brightened, making a tiny little voice inside my head scream 'Yes!'

"And you are?" I asked.

"Gallagher. Gallagher Macleod."

"You must be quite the traveler."

His left eyebrow rose. "What do ye mean, lass?"

"You know. *Gallagher's Travels* was a favorite book of mine."

He laughed, doubled over, and I squirmed. "Have I said something funny?"

"I think ye meant ye read *Gulliver's Travels*. 'Twa favorite of mine, as well."

I turned northward, frowning. Wading in a little deeper, while keeping the water from the breaking waves no higher than my own knees, he joined me.

"Apologies, lass. Couldn't help myself. May I know yer name?"

No harm in sharing, I suppose, since I doubt I'll ever see him after today. "Reagan Brownell."

He gasped, but did not laugh.

"What? Is it odd my parents named me Reagan after a former president?"

"Nay. 'Tis just that *Reagan* 'tis a popular Celtic name."

As I let his words sink in, he walked beside me, remaining between me and the safety of the shore.

The waves grew in intensity and one splashed against my side. I giggled, enjoying the silkiness of the lukewarm water that fully dampened my swimsuit up to my chest. I managed to stay on my feet while he went down on one knee. As I waited for him to stand, I spotted something light gray, round, and sparkling near my left foot.

Reaching down, I picked up the item, about four inches in diameter and nearly flat with a star-like pattern on its surface. "Look. I found a sand dollar." I'm surprised to find one in such perfect shape. This bodes well for my new life in North Carolina.

Gallagher called out to me, but I couldn't make out what he said. Moments later, a huge wave slammed into me. I tumbled under the surface, hitting my head on the sandy bottom. In surprise, I gasped and gulped a mouthful of salt water.

Before I could find the surface, large arms grabbed me under my shoulders and lifted me back onto my feet. Choking and spitting water, I tried to sweep soaking wet hair out of my face.

"If ye drowned the first time I tried swimming, it would be all me fault. Be ye well, lass?"

Gallagher gazed down at me with a worried expression. His large fingers helped clear the hair from half my face, allowing me to see. "You helped me up?"
"I admit I hesitated the moment ye fell beneath that wave, but I worried about yer safety. His hands circled my upper arms and the heat that raced up and over my entire body took my mind off my disheveled appearance.

Happily, I still clutched the sand dollar. "I'm okay. Will this scare you from enjoying the ocean?"

He chuckled and led me deeper, past the breaking waves. "I am feeling much better, knowing ye be fine. Facing me fears makes sense. Back in the Highlands I've

28

taken on angry Highland bulls or a drunken tourist, once or twice."

We suddenly stood in calm water that teased the tops of my breasts. I straightened the swimsuit fabric and glanced toward the surfers. Keeping out of their way made sense, but it sure looked like fun. Maybe I'd try my hand at surfing. Someday.

Someday? Isn't that one of the reasons I left my last boyfriend, cleared out of my New York apartment, and moved to a state I had never even visited? "I think I'll start taking surfing lessons. Maybe you can take swimming lessons at the same time? I saw a sign on the lifeguard station offering lessons."

He cocked his head, then watched a surfer fall off a small wave, then pop safely to the surface. Would he worry I might fall and not resurface if I took up such a sport? My ex never cared about my life, my wishes, nor my hopes and dreams. "It might be nice to have someone worry about me," I whispered.

The look of disbelieve on his face made me pause. His lips pressed together in a frown while his eyebrows lowered. "Why would ye think no one worried over ye? A beautiful lass like ye?" He paused, bent down, and kissed me. "My feelings for ye began the moment ye tripped over my legs and ye landed face-first into the sand. I had never seen such a disheveled specimen of American womanhood. Took great strength to hold in me laughter."
Should I laugh or cry? I look a mess with sand in my hair. Besides, he's from another country. I doubt he'll hang around.

"It's just an idea," I whispered. Looking toward the horizon the setting sun at our backs had turned the sky a deep coral.

"I like yer idea and since my plans are tied up in attending Highland games in North America, I could use a home base in this area. "Your job is wrapped up in Highland games?" Could a person make a living doing that?

"There be plenty of gatherings and festivals along the eastern coast, as ye call this area, and I earn enough competing. The paid endorsements don't hurt, either. I need a dwelling where I can lay me head. I doona enjoy hotels."

"I can suggest just the place."

"Aye? Near the ocean?"

I looked out to sea and thought about my next move. Things had changed for the better and I did, after all, just move into a lovely new apartment. There is plenty of room for a kilted handsome roommate.

Feathered Travel Time

Red-breasted robins
tap on frosty birdbaths.
Doves coo as crunchy leaves
float on crisp morning air.

Red cardinals beg for seed,
while clouds darken,
threatening rain or snow.
Say good-bye to summer.

Hummingbirds head south,
nests tumble to the earth,
empty of feathers and finches
until spring returns.

Nancy Lee Badger

Mike Rumble by day, works in Corporate America and by night morphs into a freelance writer with his own blog. He has published in Chicken Soup for the Soul: O Canada and assorted anthologies. Mike is also a Certified Professional Resume Writer (CPRW) and writes articles for 5-West magazine.

In search of 'telligent life

"Do you understand my orders??!!", the Supreme Red Cheese Martian Commander yelled through the loudspeaker into the ears of Martian #A076-925-670 as he piloted his spacecraft through outerspace that looked like nothing more than a bunch of white cake sprinkles on a piece of black construction paper. "Yes, your all-knowing gracious Supremeness, I understand your orders. I am to proceed to planet Earth and bring back a specimen of intelligent life in time to be your caddy for your 2:30pm tee-off time at the Martian Mountains Golf & Country Club." Martian A076-925-670 calmly replied, his ears burning from his superior unnecessarily yelling at me.

"Why Earth?" A-076-9335-670 said to himself as Earth came into view, "there's no intelligent life on that planet!"

As his craft broke through Earth's atmosphere shaking like a mixing bowl with cake batter and landed in what looked like a cornfield, A-076-925-670 hoped that he would be lucky enough to just find an able bodied specimen and get back to Mars before dark. Besides, he noticed how terribly humid it was as he left his craft and what these little beasts were that flew around him making a weird buzzing noise. It was then that he happened upon what looked like one of those human beings he'd been warned about while in training at the Martian Flight Academy.

"Earthing! I am here to take you back to Mars!" A-07-925-670 bellowed at a man dressed in overalls with a straw hat on his head, "Come quietly or I will use my vaporizing gun on you!"

"Earthling? I t'aint no earthling, muh name is Zeke", the man replied, "and ah can't go to no Mars."
"Why not? Do you not believe in serving His Supremeness as his golf caddy?" A-076-925-670 said putting his fists on his waist.

"I'm too busy tendin' the field here, and if in I don't get 'er done, Pa will whup my hider like a bunch of kids goin' at a birthday pinata!" Zeke said picking a few more ears of corn.

"You must come with me! You can't expect His Supremeness to carry his own clubs do you?" A-076-925-670 said starting to sweat in the hot afternoon sun.

"See that right over there, that's muh shovel, and that right there is my muh hoe to dig holes. Ain't no one can carry them except me. So if I can carry muh own tools, his Supreme Pizza Ness or whatever you call him can carry his own tools or clubs if in that's what you call them."

"We must go now! His Supremeness is waiting!" A-076-925-670 desperately said, now being overcome by the heat.

"He's waiting?? My Pa's waiting for me to get this field done and if in I don't get it done, why he'll kick my tail clean to Mars." Zeke said starting to work on a tomato patch.

"Well, that's where we're going!" A-076-928-670 said excitedly thinking the earth being had finally realized the purpose of the mission.

"Where?" Zeke asked putting some tomatoes in a basket.

"Mars!" A-076-925-670 replied happily while swatting a few mosquitoes away from his face."

"Can'r go. Too busy." Zeke rebuked before taking a big swig from a jug of water

"Look, all I want is to find a specimen of intelligent life and take it back to Mars to serve his Supremeness as a golf caddy." A-076-925-670 begged wiping a river of sweat from his forehead.

"So, it's 'telligent life you're lookin' for in these parts? Well, there ain't none of that here…and as I told you, my name is Zeke." Zeke said turning his back to get back to his chores.

As A-076-925-670 started up the stairway into his spacecraft, his uniform soaked with sweat and his brain sore from his mind-numbing talk with Zeke, he heard someone say "Hey! Just a minute!" A-076-925-670 turned around to see Zeke standing at the bottom of the stairs.

"Did you say Mars? My favorite kind of chocolate is Mars! Do they have a few bars of Mars where we're going?" Zeke said bursting a smile. "No, we don't…" A-076-925-670 said grabbing his sore head. "Oh, darn. Well I'm too busy anyhow" Zeke said turning to head back to the field.

"Well?! Was your mission a success?! Do you have a specimen of intelligent life on board to bring back to be my caddy?!" the Supreme Red Cheese Martian commander bellowed on the intercom shortly after A-076-925-670 got his spacecraft in the air and on its return voyage to Mars.

"Shut up." A-076-925-670 curtly replied before turning the intercom off and taking some Martian Migraine Strength pain pills.

It was nature

I packed up my dog and got in my car needing to drive somewhere different.
It was nature.
I drove far, looking for us to visit someplace on the outskirts of town.
It was nature.
I parked my car, leashed up my dog, and looked at the trail ahead.
It was nature.
My dog and I walked the path and he sniffed every tree.
It was nature.
I heard no noise, just the chirping of birds.
It was nature.
We sat on a bench looking at the peaceful lake through the trees.
It was nature.
My dog and I kept walking until we got so tired and I asked myself. "why can't you stop?"
It was nature.
We got back to the car and I looked back at the trail and wondered what made it so special.
It was nature.

Mike Rumble

Chanah Wizenberg received her BA from Hunter College
in English and Creative Writing. Her poetry and short
stories have appeared in several magazines and anthologies.
Chanah has been a professional ballerina, a pastry chef, and
English teacher. She resides in Raleigh, North Carolina
with her dog, Asha, and her cat, Marmalade.

Take the Power Back

"It took some doing, but we did it; we turned the tables.
Now we're in charge. Men have lost voting rights, control
over their bodies, family finances, and the right to work,"
Stella stated with a shit-eating grin spread across her face.

"Oh, they can still work," laughed Audrey, "just not
outside the home, or at any paying job. Their new job is
caring for the children, managing the household chores, as
well as preparing and serving the meals."

"Don't forget the most important part," said
Madeline. "For those of us who want children, we decide
on when and how many, one or two. The allotted amount.
More than that, we must foster or adopt. At that point, the
men are required to have a vasectomy."

"I love that part!" said Ally.
The four leaders of Take the Power Back (a group that
grew out of the need to end the takeover from the extremist
far right GOP in the last presidential election where women
lost all their rights) sat back in their chairs. All breathing a
collective sigh of relief. Today was Friday, their day to

meet at the local indie coffee shop, Rosa's Place, for breakfast.

Some people found Rosa's to be old-fashioned. There were no exposed ceiling pipes, no ugly concrete floors, bare walls, or metal tables and chairs. It was free of the incessant loud noise found in the modern eateries with an industrial look and feel to them. Those places made sure people were in and out, turning tables to make a bigger profit. At Rosa's there were round tables covered with blue checked cloth tablecloths, comfortable chairs all made from wood. Monet prints and old wooden spoons of various sizes were arranged on the walls. All this made for a comfortable dining experience, conducive to intimate conversation. Therefore, a perfect meeting place.

"I never thought we could pull it off," said Audrey, shaking her head in disbelief.

"If it weren't for the help from the International Women's Alliance, we couldn't have done it. Can you imagine the men forming a global alliance that vows to donate money to a fund for preserving the rights of women worldwide? For pledging to support women in their fight against oppression, abuse, and their right to decide their own health care. Hell no, not worldwide," said Stella. Ally wrinkled her face in disgust, "They're far too selfish for that."

"After that orange buffoon, we had no choice. It was past the time to take control," said Stella. "We flipped all the rights that he and his associates took from us. Beginning with control over our own bodies. Now men have no control over theirs."

"At last, women dominate! A new matriarchal society led by women, for women, focused on the needs of women," Ally said, smiling.

Lifting their coffee cups, the women cheered, "Hear, hear!"

The table grew quiet as the women settled into their food. As Stella ate, she reflected on their monumental achievement. It had been quite a challenge to remove The Orange Menace et al. from the presidential office. Thanks to the IWA, they did it. Through the money women donated, and continue to donate, the IWA bought and tempted corrupt politicians, and judges, plus the crime members of The Orange Menace, with deceitful promises of glory-filled days of prestige for their "public service." Nothing like using a page or two out of their playbook to win the power back for women. It was a necessary but temporary plan. A plan Stella hoped wouldn't last for too long. Their goal was a return to democracy. In fact, a better developed democratic republic. In the meantime, the convicted criminals of the previous administration were locked away for a good ten to twenty years.

"You know," started Madeline, bringing Stella out of her deep thoughts, "does anyone feel guilty? I mean, there are good men out there who were on our side. They supported us."

Stella regained her focus, "Think of it as them taking one for the team. Remember the plan. The aim is to target the extreme right individuals for about four to five years. They must go through the same experiences that we've gone through as women under extreme patriarchy of the GOP led by The Orange Menace. Once they understand

how wrong it is to have to control over a specific population, denying them their freedoms as American citizens; we'll return to the table to renegotiate for a fair society, restoring our country to a democratic republic."
Madeline pushed the food around her plate. "Four to five years is a long time for those good men to wait."
With an edge to her voice Stella looked Madeline in the eye, "remind yourself how long it took us to get the right to vote, the right to have our own bank account, the…"

"Okay, okay!" Madeline cut in.
Audrey swallowed a big bite of her scrambled egg. Clearing her throat, to redirect the conversation back to the topic, "don't forget their women too. Many of those husbands' wives agree with them. It's important that they learn how their men have taken advantage of them."

"Do you think they will?" asked Ally.

"Will what?" asked Stella, taking her eyes off Madeline's.

"Do you think they'll come to realize that having control over another individual's body is not right?"

"Yeah," agreed Madeline, relieved the focus had shifted from her. "What if they never come around?"

"That's a good question. We need to think about that. It's likely some won't," Stella agreed, "but for right now, we can enjoy our newfound power, asserting dominance. Don't forget we have the exams in place. From now on, anyone aspiring to hold office, including senators, congresspeople; even the presidency candidates must pass the competency tests. They have to demonstrate comprehension of our government's workings, familiarity

with the Bill of Rights, the Constitution, civil rights, and a grasp of our forefathers' history," said Stella.
Heads bobbed up and down, around the table. "Having those in place now is such a relief," Audrey said. "We can regain control of our educational system." The others nodded in agreement.

"They'll have earned their positions through the high standards they must pass to become teachers. We have achieved success in standardizing the curriculum nationwide. All students receive equal education, including civics, from kindergarten through twelfth grade. No more sugar-coated history. It's also age appropriate," Madeline emphasized.

"Everyone has worked hard to achieve these goals. We've been planning for years. We must continue to stay strong. It's no time to become lax," said Stella.
Again, the women nodded.

As the women quieted, their focus shifted from talking to enjoying their food. Just as they were finishing, there was a commotion in the street. Someone was yelling obscenities. The women, in reflex, looked towards the noise.

"What on earth?" started Madeline, "Duck!" Madeline, Ally, Audrey, Stella all dove under the table.

"What did you see?" asked Ally, her breath coming it quick gasps.
The sound of glass shattering provided an answer to her question, accompanied by a muffled explosion, the smell of smoke, screams of terror among igniting flames.

"Oh crap! Someone threw a Molotov cocktail in here; we've got to get out!" shouted Stella.

"Which way?" Audrey, her voice an octave higher than normal.

The sounds of panic and terror filled Rosa's Place as patrons rushed to escape, pushing, shoving, knocking people down in their frantic race towards the front door. The smoke grew dense as the flames licked the tablecloths, setting fire to the clothing of some customers who couldn't escape the engulfed tables, causing their screams to intensify

"Back door," choked Stella, "we've got to find the way out."

"Through the kitchen then," coughed Ally, regaining her composure, "come on, follow me."

Almost blinded from the smoke, the women covered their mouths by pulling up their blouses or shirts. Coughing, eyes watering from the smoke, they followed Ally as best they could.

They wound their way through the kitchen, almost empty of staff, who bailed after hearing the commotion out front. The fire alarms piercing the din. The air was better here, as the smoke hadn't yet reached the kitchen.

"Uh, I can breathe," said Madeline, taking a huge breath.

"Yes," agreed Audrey, wiping the tears from her eyes with trembling hands.
After the remaining staff headed out the door, Ally gestured for the women to keep moving. Once outside, they breathed a collective sigh of relief.

"Oh, my god!" said Ally, her breathing just short of hyperventilating. "That was, was terrifying."
The women huddled together, "anyone catch what that man was yelling? I mean, aside from his cursing?" asked Stella, rubbing her still stinging eyes.

"No, it was too garbled," said Madeline, hugging herself around the middle as if she had a stomachache. "I've never been this scared."

"Hey," said one of the kitchen staff coming over to them, "I'm Gary. Do you know what happened? What were they throwing?"

"Molotov cocktails. I think he threw several into the shop."

There were sirens sounding in the distance, growing closer.

"The fire department's coming," said Audrey. "The police should be coming, too."

"Man, that was scary. I'll bet he's angry over the takeover. No offense meant," Gary said, glancing at the women, "things are pretty harsh for us guys now."

The women looked at one another but said nothing. Ally nodded in understanding. Madeline began wringing her hands. Audrey plucked at a loose thread on her blouse. Gary stood, staring at the bakery, smoke seeping from the back door. "What do I do now? I need my job."

"I'm so sorry, you should be able to get unemployment until they re-open," Ally said, tucking a loose hair behind her ear, again and again.

"You mean, if they re-open," said Gary, hanging his head. He trudged back to his fellow workers.

The women grew quiet. "We knew there'd be repercussions," said Madeline, her tone subdued, "but such violence? I was hoping it wouldn't happen. Wishful thinking on my part."

"I think we've all been hanging on to a pink cloud about that," said Stella. As she spoke, she placed her hand over her heart, pressing hard. Her one tell, that she was stressed. "It's time for us to face it. We need to be careful. It's dangerous times ahead."

"Let's go around front. Where did everyone park?" asked Audrey, wondering if anyone besides her had parked close to Rosa's. "Hope our cars are ok."

"I had to park a couple of blocks away. I should be ok," said Madeline.

"Me, too," said Stella.

"Oh, I parked right out front!" worried Ally.

"Let's step on it then," Stella said, still clutching her hand to her heart.

When they reached the front of the building, police had sealed off the entire block with crime scene tape. The place was swarming with police and firefighters.
Audrey asked Ally, "Can you see your car?"

"Uh," straining to see, "oh, yes. There's debris, but I don't see any physical damage."

"That's good, Ally. Sure hope no one got seriously hurt," said Madeline.

"Hey, there! Where'd you ladies come from? You need to get behind the tape right now." A police officer, heavyset, with a red face, shouted, "you're in a secured area!"

44

"Sorry officer, will do," said Stella, "by the way we were in the shop when that man threw the Molotov cocktails."

"Oh, well uh, come see me first, then get behind the tape."

The officer took their statements. There was a tense moment when he asked them why they were in the coffee shop. Until now, they had concealed their IWA affiliation and membership with Take the Power Back group. That personal question caused one frightening moment. If he found out, they'd be arrested. Charged with seditious conspiracy among other things. Stella wondered if someone had overheard their conversation, mentioning it to him. Madeline recovered first. "Why we were just having our social breakfast to catch up on the week's gossip, is all. We girls have our day out on Fridays."

"I see, just a fun day out to talk girl stuff, no plotting with the Take the Power Back then?"

"Oh no, not us," continued Madeline, feigning shock. "Those women are men-haters, not us."

"Don't get me started on those fools," said Ally.

"You know that's right," agreed Audrey.

Officer George studied each woman. Madeline put her hands behind her back, holding them together as tight as she could to prevent herself from wringing them. Likewise, Audrey held her purse closer so she wouldn't pick at the loose thread. Ally was biting her nails. Only Stella remained motionless, afraid to breathe, her hand over heart as if she were going to say the Pledge of Allegiance.

"You ladies, ok? You're looking kind of nervous."

"Uh, yes, it's just that what happened was frightening. It's hitting me how close we came to getting hurt, or, or worse," Audrey said, her voice quivering. George looked back at the burning store, then back towards the women. "Yeah, you're right. Ever since the big change, some guys are losing it. Can't blame 'em myself. This country's goin' to pot. I've got your information and statements. If we need anything else, we'll contact you," George walked away, mumbling about the women in charge of our nation.

It's been five years since the takeover. The violence ebbed. Instead of daily protests, there were scant few per month. Most men complied with the new order of things. Stella, Audrey, Madeline, along with Ally, met up at Rosa's. The owner has since renovated the shop, making improvements. It still had the same welcoming feel, but now had bookshelves lining the walls, with one wall dedicated to displays of art by local artists. Soft classical music played in the background. Even though it was bigger, it still had a cozy atmosphere.

"I got word from the White House. They've already set things in motion to reinstate a democratic republic," Stella said. "They're going to set up groups all over the country. Two women from each chapter of Take the Power Back will facilitate these groups. We'll keep a tally of those who continue to oppose equal rights."
Madeline interrupted, "Wait, only those who're against equal rights?"

"Yes."

"Why?" asked Ally. "What are they going to do with the list?"

"They say these folks are to be treated with extra care. The plan is to mandate them into classes to educate them on why it's to everyone's benefit to have an equal society."

"I'm not sure about that," said Audrey. "It sounds like reprogramming."

"I know it does. The president assures me it's not that."

"You believe her?" asked Ally, eyeing the others to see if they were as concerned as she was about the "program." Their eyes were glued to Stella's awaiting her answer.

"I do," finished Stella.

"Okay then," said Ally, as she began to twirl her hair around her finger.

With feelings of trepidation, the other women acquiesced. Stella took out her phone, "I'm emailing you the guidelines; topics for discussions that include questions to ask, the attendance plus tally sheets. Although voluntary, we must note the men, the women too, who don't attend the meetings. Those people will receive a survey asking them why they chose not to attend. We hope to find another means of reaching them."

"Quite the daunting task," said Madeline, opening her beeping phone.

"Yes, it is," Audrey said, fishing for her phone in purse as it sang, "Who Let the Dogs Out," her ringtone announcing a new email.

"We can do it," began Ally, already looking at her email, "as long as we stay focused."
The women quieted as they read the email, examining the topics of discussion and questions.

"These are good. They should inspire discussion, making, I hope, the members of these groups feel a new connection as American citizens. One with an understanding of what makes our country different from others; our freedom to choose," said Madeline. Each woman nodded, a small smile appearing at the corners of their mouths.

"At last," Ally said, "genuine hope is in sight to regain our democracy."

The women had congregated on the roof of Rosa's, along with the other patrons. The joyful, celebratory mood was infectious. Down below, the parade marched along with the award-winning high school band playing Stars and Stripes Forever.

"Ten years. It took us ten years, but we did it," said Stella, a smile lighting up her face as she raised her glass of champagne.

"Yes, ten long years," agreed Madeline. "I wasn't sure we'd succeed."

"But we did," Audrey said, raising her glass with the others. "The entire country is celebrating. How perfect is that? Reclaiming our democracy on July 4th?"

"It doesn't get any better! Three cheers for democracy!" Ally said.

"Hip, hip hooray! Hip, hip hooray! Hip, hip hooray!" the women chorused, then drained their glasses. It was a long, glorious night of celebration

It was a week later the sound of Glory, Glory Hallelujah playing on her phone awakened Stella, the ring tone for Take the Power Back, "Oh my god! Turn on the news right now! It's awful, just awful," sobbed Madeline.

"What? Madeline? Did someone die?" her head pounding from coming to from a dead asleep. "Tell me, what's wrong?"

"Just turn on the TV. Those tallies we did for men clinging to racist, bigoted views? They lied to us! They killed the ones who didn't change."

"What do you mean?" Stella asked, as she made her way to the living room to turn on the news, massaging her neck as she went, to quell her mounting headache. "Are you talking about those missing people?"

"Yes, I knew there was something fishy. We heard about it once on the news. Then nothing. They were k-, they're all dead! The administration had them killed. The bastards covered it up, keeping it out of the press." Madeline hiccupped through her sobs.
The news anchor for CNN was playing a recording of the president ordering the deaths of all the people who didn't agree with equal rights laws. It couldn't be, but there it was. No mistake. Stella, along with the women in TPB, had been part of the scheme for murder! Stella collapsed onto the couch, a knot in her stomach, her heart, a deep hurt within.

"Madeline, we are a part of it! I can't believe it. She lied to us. Audrey was right. How could I have been so naïve?"

"I think we all were, Stella," said Madeline, sniffing now, "I feel sick about it."

"Me too. Have you heard from the others?"

"Not yet. What do we do?"

"I-I don't know. Maybe everyone should come to my place where we can talk in private."

"Okay, I'll call them. We'll be there in an hour." Madeline hung up on Stella before she could respond.

"Shit, shit, shit," cursed Stella as pulled herself up off the couch to get dressed, skipping her shower.

Once dressed, she went into autopilot mode, preparing coffee and popping frozen croissants into the oven to have them ready for when the others arrived. She placed a tray with small plates, napkins, a couple of mini spatulas for the jam, and butter. Next to the tray, she left room for the croissants. Beside the coffee, she put cream, sugar, and Stevia for Ally, who doesn't take sugar.

As the women arrived, Stella greeted them with a hug. No one spoke. They served themselves coffee and croissants before finding a seat in the living room. Nobody sipped coffee, no one ate any croissants. There they sat, a heavy silence weighing them down.
Stella broke the silence, "I'm sorry I dismissed your concern about the tallies. I'm to blame. It's my fault. I should have known better. How could I have been such a fool?"

"No, Stella, it's not yours alone. We all took part. We trusted the president. All of us, all over the entire country!" wailed Audrey.

The was room still again. Stella looked from face to face. What was she seeing there? Fear? Yes, fear. She felt it too, deep in her heart. Absently, she placed her hand over her heart.

Breaking the silence Madeline asked, "do you suppose they'll come for us?"

Her voice flat, Ally responded, "we led the groups, we wrote the tallies."

"I don't know," said Stella, in a monotone, "our names were on those tallies.

Chanah Wizenberg

Dorothy La Motta has published children's books, romance, fiction, non-fiction and poetry. Her work is featured in multiple anthologies, and the North Carolina Historical and Literary Journals. She holds membership in Triangle East Writers, Triangle Association of Freelancers, North Carolina Writers Network and Triangle East Chamber of Commerce.

Fly, Baby, Fly

I was sipping my 'good to the last drop' of Maxwell House coffee when I heard my German exchange student Romy, bolting down the stairs unusually early and very excited about something. "Okay, I said curiously, "why are you so happy this early in the morning?" She giggled. "Ms. Dot," she replied in a soft, sweet tone, "could we do something really exciting outside the state of North Carolina before I go home to Germany next week?" She surprised me. But then I realized everything I did for her amazing cultural journey of fun and educational activities in America were indeed only in North Carolina.

Feeling a twinge of guilt, I said, "Sure, I promise I'll find another adventure you will never forget." So, off I went to consult the airwaves of wonder while she munched on a bagel topped with Nutella and a mug of hot chocolate melting her mini marshmallows. I wanted this last-ditch effort to be exhilarating with just a touch of risk involved. Teens love risky activities.

After ten minutes of playing Sherlock Holmes on the web
and searching for unusual adventures, what did my
wondering eyes see across the screen? Indoor Skydiving!
Whoa, I just hit the jackpot! Overjoyed by my fabulous
find, I asked my neighbor's exchange student, Poopae,
from Thailand if she would like to join us. Need I say
more?

With their parent's permission, we ventured North under
sunny skies and warm gentle breezes. Two hours later, we
arrived in Virginia Beach, Virginia. The salty smell of the
ocean greeted us and awakened our nostrils as we all took
deep breaths filling our lungs with clean, fresh air. Seagulls
circled overhead squawking their discontent with us for
ignoring their begging antics for morsels of any kind.

Once inside, the huge glass dome enveloped nearly the
whole interior of the building. The girls almost collided
getting to the signup counter. While I waited for their
registration to be processed, my eyes scanned flying,
pretend astronauts twirling in circles, floating, diving, and
twisting upward to the top of the dome. They were playing
in space, defying gravity, and making memories. The girls
could barely control their excitement.

"Miss Dot" shouted Romy, you should do this too, it will
be fun." "Are you kidding?" I gasped. "I'm 80 years old," I
blurted out trying not to sound as frightened as I felt. They
both giggled again and promptly took each of my arms and

escorted me to the signup counter. They weren't taking 'no'
for an answer. I must admit, curiosity took
me hostage and I reluctantly surrendered to this outlandish
challenge.

Moments later, we three compadres and other adventurous
humans of all ages, were sitting in a brief training session
to learn the basics of body flight, aerodynamics, how to
maintain stability, and correct body position in the vertical
wind tunnel. It didn't sound too bad until the instructor told
us that the wind inside the tunnel would be a hurricane
speed of about 85 to 95 miles per hour for us to become
'airborne.' Some young guys laughed, others dropped
their jaws, and Romy and Poopae's eyes bulged a little.

I was getting excited about trying something new, but at
that hurricane speed I worried more about my wig flying
off, my dentures getting pulled out, my contacts blowing
back to North Carolina, and my eardrums bursting. But I
was too embarrassed to disappoint the kids.

As NASA would say, 'It's all systems go,' and no backing
out now. We were fitted with colorful, authentic-looking
flight suits, helmets with a snug chin strap, goggles, and
earplugs. Ahhh! Wig safe, dentures safe, contacts safe, and
eardrums safe! I'm ready for takeoff. I could feel 'the kid'
in me screaming to come out and show the younger
generation just how cool I really was. Even though I'm 80,
I didn't want to waste the precious years I have left
wishing and hoping I had done the exciting things I was
still able to do, and didn't.

Romy bravely stepped inside the noisy wind tunnel first as
the instructor gripped the leg pockets of the flight suit to
help with 'liftoff.' Another wind master outside the dome
controlled the oncoming hurricane and Wham! They were
both airborne. Within seconds, Romy was flying in the air,
circling the dome like a 747 Jet awaiting landing
instructions.

Next, Poopae's petite body spiraled upward almost to the
top of the dome with her pig-tails
flying in opposite directions. My heart skipped a beat as
she nose-dived, circled, and recoiled before she ended her
short flight time.

I was next. Though Romy and Poopae cheered me on, I still
felt my heart racing as my wisdom and common sense were
at war with my adventurous childish side. The 'kid' in me
won. I stepped cautiously into the wind tunnel. The spooky,
deep roar of the invisible wind mesmerized me. The
instructor gripped the pockets of my flight suit. I leaned
forward, arms extended out and curved slightly inward,
legs straight out, and head and body facing downward.
I wanted to curl my legs up but remembered in training that
if I did that, I would plummet to the rubberized elastic
floor. I thought to myself, this is what you might look like
after being run over by a tractor-trailer.

I chuckled as the initial burst of the forceful wind startled
me. I wanted to put my hands in front of my face to block
the windy intruder from pushing my cheeks upward until I

realized I was getting a free facial massage. The roar of the
wind would muffle my screams anyway, so I just embraced
the force and tried not to crumble to the floor like a
speeding meteor from outer space.

I was experiencing the thrill of skydiving without an
airplane or parachute. I felt like an aircraft and an
astronaut! My arms were the wings, my head the cockpit,
my body the cabin, and my legs the tail section. I was an
awesome granny-flying machine!

One minute came and went and I was now being carefully
and gently brought down to earth in a standing position as
the wind subsided to a gentle breeze. What an experience!
I'm not bragging….(Yes I am) but I can't wait to do this
again with my grandkids.

We each received a "Certified Flight Certificate' for
bragging purposes along with pictures in our astronaut
flight suits. We celebrated with lunch on the beach scarfing
down giant shrimp Po-Boy subs, a stroll on the beach with
the foamy ocean tickling our toes and massaging our
feet, followed by a little souvenir shopping. With sand in
our shoes, smiles on our faces, and memories planted in our
hearts, we headed home to North Carolina for a delicious
dinner of southern BBQ ribs, sweet tea, and corn on the
cob.

A wonderful thing happened that day. I kept my promise
and gave two foreign exchange students the time of their
lives 'outside' North Carolina. No matter how old we are,

we all have a 'little kid' inside us bursting to come out at just the right time, the right place, and when the right opportunity presents itself. I didn't let my age stop me from being a teenager again, and I overcame my initial fear and anxiety while having the blast of my life when I stepped outside my comfort zone to try something new. . . . . Ziplining next!!

Autumn's Debut

Every season has its own beauty and charm
No more winter blues, or steamy summer days
It's a special time of year to savor nature at its best
Fall is a time for hiking and paddling on serene lakes

And having fun leaving ripples behind your strokes
Biking on leaf-strewn paths, crunching them into crumbs
Not a day of boredom in between
Colorful gourds twist and turn into comical shapes

Apple cider, candy apples, apple dumplings,
Apple turnovers and apple sauce
If you're not dreaming of apples,
You must be eating them

Homemade jams and jellies tantalize your taste buds
Cucumbers wait patiently to enter the briny broth
That makes your lips pucker up at the first snap of a
Seasoned cucumber transformed into pickle heaven

My Moment in Time

The early morning sunrise was a rainbow
of blues, purples, and pinks spread across the horizon
I stood on a cliff near Lake Ontario relishing the
wonder of God as He woke me early, while He
kept others sleeping

The morning chill sent shivers down my spine as I
huddled under my fleece jacket. I was alone with God
as the lake's water gently rippled in the breeze
No one was walking on the beach
Neighbors were still sleeping

I then heard a squawking from a nearby bird
I was no longer alone
I looked up expecting to see a seagull
But God gave me more
As the squawking got louder, my eyes raised
to the heavens and my morning gift was to witness
hundreds of Canada geese in a 'V' formation
it was a Michelangelo painting in the sky
Not one bird was out of formation or lagging behind
The lead goose was big and strong,
his feathers rippled in the air
They were 'perfection in flight'
Where's my camera when I need it?

I wanted to shout to my family to wake up and see this
beautiful sight. But I stood still…just me and God, and his
amazing feathered creatures

It was God's gift to me that early morning. He wrapped
it not in a box with a bow, but in his rainbow sunrise
reflecting off a shimmering mirror lake
The squawking was his way of saying 'Good Morning'
to me through his geese. The fly-over delighted my soul

Sometimes we don't need others around us.
It was my moment in time.
I thanked God for my eyesight, my hearing,
and his wonderful surprise gift as I stood motionless on the
cliff surrounded by the beauty his fingers made and gladly
absorbed the miracle that was meant for only me.

My heart was pounding with joy as a tear cascaded down
my cheek
My smile widened in gratefulness to the God who loves me
and sent me this unexpected gift just for . . . .
. . . .my moment in time.

The Blank Page

The deadline is approaching fast
My pen and paper await my command
I try to focus, but fog enters my brain
I focus again but to no avail

I leave my table to sit at my computer
Waiting for it to talk to me
The dreaded blank screen stares at me,
mocks me and laughs at me

It dares me to strike my keyboard
to break the deadly silence
I stare back in retaliation
I grit my teeth, clench my fist

I refuse to surrender defeat to the black abyss
I twirl my fingers to ready them to pound
One hour passes… my index finger controls
The scroll bar on the right of the screen

Just to see some action…any action
Even the pointy-nose triangle has
A beginning and an end
Why can't I?

I inhale a deep breath and relax
A clear idea is beginning to form
Words are bouncing around in my head
Like a rubber ball escaping the grip of a child

I strike a key, then another, then another
The silence is finally broken
Words flow from my mind to my fingers
To the keyboard, to the dreaded blank page

Now dotted with words that were held captive
Waiting to escape the cranium prison of death
The jungle of once mindless fleeting thoughts
Has given birth to a delightful story

Dorothy La Motta

Marvis Henderson-Daye is a member of the Triangle Association of Freelancers. This is her fourth submission for TAF Anthologies. In addition, she published Nine Lives, Every Storm Runs Out of Rain, and a children's series, Grandmomma M. When she is not writing, she is dancing across the world.

Blessed and Highly Favored

Every day, I try to stick to my 'am' routine. I stretch, deep breathe, hydrate, give gratitude during my devotion, and set my day with intention. This routine allows my body and soul to wake up. For a person who used to suffer from panic attacks in her sleep, this routine changed her life.

During Dr. Shana's Zoom presentation on what an 'am' routine was in the middle of the pandemic, I was stressed out. The world shut down, and my government contract abruptly ended. I was also battling to finish my doctoral journey as quickly as possible because the loans had doubled. Although I was skeptical about the routine working, I was desperate. My body hurt in places that I thought were impossible to hurt. And while I was afraid of the future, I was more afraid that my history of insomnia and pain was returning.

Stretching, deep breathing, and hydration were easy to incorporate into my new morning routine. Devotions that included gratitude and setting my days with intention were difficult. The idea of reading a daily devotion caused me to procrastinate in creating the 'am' routine. So, I adjusted the routine. Instead of reading the devotions, I listened to music. As I rummaged through old CDs, I uncovered a one-hour CD with uplifting gospel music.

The other difficult step in the new routine was setting my days with intention. I created my routine during COVID. People were still wearing masks and debating whether to take the vaccines. With a compromised immune system and the added stress from the doctoral journey, each day was chaotic and unpredictable. Yet, I needed to set a realistic schedule My doctoral program was also online. Instead of speeding up the doctoral journey, the process slowed to a snail's pace. During that time, I lost my cool, calm demeanor as I waited for responses from my dissertation committee members. One of the many university's standard operating procedures was that each dissertation committee member had fifteen business days to respond to emails and make changes to the proposal and the dissertation. So, to overcome my frustration with that process, I created other opportunities for my line dance community to enjoy.

To stay sane at the onset of the pandemic, I became proficient with Zoom! I had line dance classes, virtual book club meetings, pajama parties, birthday celebrations, virtual cookouts, virtual Bingo, and fundraisers! I also attended virtual meetings and festivals I could not afford before COVID.

As I implemented the changes to create my 'am' routine, I noticed that I struggled with unhappiness and uncertainty. I acknowledged those feelings because I felt unworthy to have a life full of love, laughter, and fun. Because the pandemic created uncertainty in my life, I felt I had no control. Instead of gratitude, I focused on what I did not have. So, to overcome those feelings, I had to conduct an internal mindset reset to create the changes in my routine and become that fun-loving person I wanted to be.

I began the changes to the 'am' routine by making the easier changes. Before I left bed each morning, I stretched and began my deep breathing exercises because I realized I held my breath when I became tense. Whether or not I was going back to sleep, I refreshed my drink and played the CD. Even when I woke up in the middle of the night, I played that CD! Each song prepared me to overcome my life challenges during the implementation stages of the devotional and intentional setting steps.

One of the songs, Hold On, encouraged me to not give up on my dreams. And I admit, there were several times when I was ready to give up on the doctorate. I was so angry with one of the members of my dissertation committee that my hood was bubbling out of me, and at some point, I was going to cuss her out. Where I came from, I learned to use bad words from some of the best lyricists. In one sentence, they could use those bad words as adjectives, nouns, verbs, and adverbs. Can you imagine how some words would feel when used as verbs? During that time, I had to listen to the gospel CD twice in the morning because I intended to cuss out somebody before the end of the day! I was and continue to be a work in progress.

I realized my mindset was changing as I continued implementing my 'am' routine. Another song, Blessed and Highly Favored, became my mantra. I became grateful for the good, the bad, and the ugly! So, while battling the university, my house started falling apart. My home was almost 20 years old, which in house years equates to ancient. The garage door springs snapped. Then, the water heater sprung a leak. Thankfully, I had an app where I could hire professionals to fix the problems.

Because of my new 'am' routine, I gave thanks because I found affordable professionals who fixed my home. If only I had a professional to fix my dissertation committee member. While another committee member could not fix the other member, he stepped in to advocate for me. Our first meeting to resolve the issues with the dissertation was tense. Because I used my Apple computer, I could see the text messages in the upper right corner of the screen. When the aggravating committee member chastised me, I saw two things. One thing that I saw was red because of my blinding rage! The other thing I saw was a message in the upper right corner of the screen that said, "Hold on." I do not believe in coincidences, so I shut my mouth and waited. The issues were resolved, and I graduated.

Now, I believe and know that I am blessed and highly favored. While my faith is constantly tested, my 'am' routine has grounded me to accept those challenges with grace and gratitude. For example, Dr. Henderson-Daye had student loans to repay once I graduated! Fortunately, the US Department of Education (Department of Ed) investigated the university, and the university was charged the largest fine from the US Department of Ed for misrepresenting the costs and structure of their online degrees. When the US Department of Ed called me, I stumbled, and my faith wavered. My friends could not understand my apprehension. So, I explained that the government investigation had begun before they called you. And when the government says they will accommodate your availability to speak with them, you schedule the time and pray for the best outcome.

And, Lord, did I pray! If I had fought and graduated earlier, I would not have qualified for three student loan forgiveness programs. I asked for guidance to determine which program would erase the debt. Then, I used every degree I earned to complete and submit the documentation. Wow, when those loans were forgiven, I knew I was blessed.

Within a month of the US Department of Education's call, my house sprung a leak! My master bath and master closet had to be gutted and repaired. For four months, I was in construction hell! While my faith was intact, I was reverting to my hood education. My 'am' routine saved the construction supervisor's life. Once a friend stepped in, the repairs were completed.

As I set my days with intention, I also learned to speak what I wanted into existence. When I stopped relying on my understanding and gave the stumbling blocks and battles to the Lord, I received better than I imagined. Thus far, I have ridden a camel in my high heels and climbed (got on an elevator) the tallest building in the world!

Although my contract was renewed, the school district closed the school, which displaced my students. I was furious! I am still a work in progress. So, I asked my principal if she wanted to go out with a whimper or a bang. As she rolled her eyes, she said a bang! With the support of my line dance community members, we held the first and last Red-Carpet Dancing with the Stars Ball!

The line dance community members donated dresses. My disc jockey played the music. The staff decorated the gym with star backdrops and a picture of the ropes and red carpet. And for a dramatic effect, the participants walked on the red carpet to enter the gym. With the PTO support, we fed two hundred people pizzas, chips, cookies, and drinks. It was an incredible sight to see my kindergarten to fifth graders dressed up and having fun. After I changed into my ball gown, one of my first graders, dressed in his white suit, escorted me on the red carpet. Looking at the gigantic grin on his face, I know he will fondly remember his experience.

I continue to speak about what I want in the universe. And so far, it has worked. I gave thanks when I won two tickets from the local radio station to a blues and jazz festival I wanted to attend. My son said he was attending Beyonce's concert in Chicago. Yep, I was in the house! While I fought the university, TAF allowed me to continue writing! I contributed two essays and one short story for TAF anthologies. I also published my first children's series, Grandmomma M!

What did I learn from this process that I want to share with you? I can still be a work in progress, blessed, and highly favored. I acknowledge my strengths and weaknesses. I share my strengths with those people that need my services.

Regarding my weaknesses, I am constantly learning and practicing patience. I fail more than succeed. I also created a personal board of directors with experts who keep me out of trouble. More importantly, I get up each morning using my 'am' routine, which makes me eager to start my day because I am blessed and highly favored.

Marvis Henderson-Daye

Cindy Brookshire is a regional representative for North Carolina Writers' Network and advisor to Triangle East Writers. Her books include A Heart for Selma: 12 Stories of Activate Selma NC; Little Towns; and (as contributing writer) Johnston County Creates: 50 Years of Creativity. She coordinates weekly Activate Selma meetings and Telling Our Stories sessions at the Harrison Center for Active Aging in Selma, North Carolina.

Moments of Dis-Grace

In Sunday School, Pastor poses the question:
How do you get into heaven? He plays
an old audio recording so we can ponder
Sister Rosetta singing about trouble nobody knows.

Her deep voice sends me reeling back
into trouble I caused, not trouble I've seen.
My moments of dis-grace rising,
swelling over like sourdough forgotten
under a damp kitchen towel:
The waitress I left without a tip
when she was working her way through college.
The coworker whose snack I stole.
The old lady from the beauty parlor
who soiled herself in a bathroom stall,
and cried out while I ran, gagging from the smell.
The car side mirror I hit, left dangling

while I went into a shop to write a note.
The driver left while I was gone; I should have stayed.
Petty gossip I spread that snapped back
changing a friend's life path.

Sister's song was only minutes, but my sins
overflowed like trash pickup after a holiday,
all the emptiness, excess, and shameful waste
set to the curb for all to see. No way I can push
that heavy heaven door open and squeeze in.
Not unless other people's sins discount mine
Like drug store coupons, ribboning at checkout:
Save ten percent for the boy who called me fat
in front of my teenage daughter? Free item Friday
for the professor who came to class drunk
and said my writing was crap,
wounding me for years?

No one came out of Sister's song clean. We all were
stone quiet in the parish hall, while Pastor
poured a pitcher of warm water into a pan, knelt,
and began washing our feet, one by one.

Cindy Brookshire

Lauren Clemmons is a published author based in Raleigh, North Carolina. Her essays, poetry, and fiction appear in anthologies, including TAF publications.

Harry the Frog, A Children's Story

In a world hidden from humans, a frog named Harry lived in a blue pond beside a fairy castle. Harry liked his home. He liked the fairies. They were fluttery and energetic. Every flutter of their wings filled the air with the scent of jasmine, or cinnamon, or mint. Harry especially liked the fairy princess, Adelyna Goldust. Every day after breakfast she fluttered about kissing frogs in ponds, frogs on logs, and frogs on rocks. Why did she kiss frogs?

Mr. Hedgehog, an avid reader, told Harry that certain frogs turn into a handsome fairy prince when kissed by a fairy princess. Mr. Hedgehog, who thought Harry's name was spelled "H-a-i-r-y", theorized that Harry might be one of those frogs. Mr. Hedgehog reasoned that Harry's name indicated a predisposition to acquiring fairy features, such as hair. If Adelyna kissed Harry enough times, then Harry might grow hair on his head and turn into a prince.

Harry pondered the hedgehog's interesting theory. Harry would very much like to become a fairy prince and spend time with Adelyna flying and fluttering about the woods among the trees and ferns. Harry also thought he would like the feeling of her warm soft lips on his frog cheek. That night, Harry dreamt of warm, soft princess kisses.

For the next two days, Harry sunbathed on his lily pad and frog-paddled about the pond trying to catch the Adelyna's attention. The princess did not notice Harry. Her attention was focused on three frogs on a log. She kissed them each repeatedly, over fifty times, with no results. The three became so embarrassed by her failed efforts that they hopped away.

While Harry watched the princess, her three cats frolicked to the pond and sat at its edge meowing. Harry hid under his lily pad. The princess's kitties meowed about the dragon chef at the Fork-n-Spoon Diner, who cooked amazing hotdogs with his flame-breath. The fairy princess now ate lunch there every day.

Still dreaming of a warm, soft kiss from the princess, Harry decided to go to the diner, order a flame-cooked hotdog, and sit with princess Adelyna. If he talked to her she might kiss him. Harry put on a nice shirt and clean pants and jumped over to the diner.

The friendly gnome diner owner greeted Harry at the door and seated him at the counter beside Adelyna, who smiled at Harry. He smiled back. The dragon chef served them each a flame-cooked hotdog. Harry and Adelyna ate lunch and talked.

After they finished talking about things that frogs and fairy princesses talk about, the princess leaned forward. Harry bubbled with enthusiasm over the warm, soft kiss he was about to receive. Adelyna kissed Harry on the cheek.

Rather than being soft and warm, the kiss was damp. Harry was crushed. His enthusiasm melted into disappointment. Adelyna, however, was not aware of Harry's disappointment. She thought her kiss was perfectly wonderful and was eager to give Harry more of them.

Adelyna invited Harry to eat lunch with her every day at the diner. Harry did not think he could decline the invitation so he accepted. Every day for countless days Harry ate lunch with Adelyna. Every day for countless days they ate dragon-flamed-cooked hotdogs. Every day for countless days Adelyna gave Harry a damp kiss. Every day for countless days Harry was disappointed.

Harry felt so heavy from hotdogs and disappointment that he could hardly jump anymore. Harry's disappointment became soft anger, which became desperation and then exasperation.

Exasperated by the countless damp kisses, Harry finally lost his patience. They had just finished eating their hotdogs. As Adelyna leaned forward to kiss his cheek, Harry held up his hand and stopped her. "My lovely, kind fairy princess," he began, "I am greatly distressed by your damp kisses and no longer wish to receive them. I have gained too much weight eating all these flame-cooked hotdogs and desire to end our lunch dates. The conversation has been most interesting and enjoyable but frankly I prefer swimming in my pond to receiving these damp kisses."

Instantly, Harry regretted his words. Adelyna's smile disappeared and her lower lip began to tremble. No one had ever criticized and rejected her kisses. She began rapidly fluttering her lustrous wings. As they fluttered, they emitted the scent of cow dung. The dragon-chef dropped a plate of hotdogs in alarm. Adelyna began to cry. Her tears were brown and slimy. Soon the entire counter was dripping with them. The more she cried the worse the smell became. The diner smelled like a hot, swampy cow pasture. Harry looked at the other diners. No one moved or spoke. The stench had frozen them into little resin figurines. It was awful. The power of cow dung had been unleashed.

"I'm sorry! Stop crying! What's happening?" croaked Harry, in terrified distress.

At that exact moment, Mr. Hedgehog entered the diner. He was EMT-certified in fairy disasters. He pulled out his pocket-sized, "Fairy Emergency Handbook Training Manual. " Page ten stated, "A fairy princess emits cow dung smells when upset and crying. A fairy princess is only upset when her countless kisses fail to unleash the magic to turn a frog into a prince and the frog finally rejects her." He further read, "Causes of failed frog-to-prince efforts include but are not limited to eating dragon flame-cooked hotdogs prior to delivering the kiss. Flame-cooked hotdogs cause damp kisses which lead to deep-seated frog disappointments. Frogs are known to desire warm soft kisses and to become exasperated when they don't receive them." The fairy internet suggested various home remedies to prevent damp kisses and the ensuing disaster, none of which Mr. Hedgehog gave much credence, except one— "an apple a day keeps the cow dung at bay."

"Ah, yes," thought Mr. Hedgehog, "use the apple to counteract the flame-cooked hotdog damp kiss effect. A classic, simple and practical approach."

Fortunately, the diner menu included fruit. Mr. Hedgehog grabbed an apple from the crate on the counter and held it to Adelyna's mouth, now covered in torrents of brown slime. "Take a bite of this apple, my fairy princess."

Adelyna's attempts to bite the apple through the slime were horrific and gory. Harry turned away. He could not watch. Finally, Harry heard a crunch. And another and another until the crunching stopped. Mr. Hedgehog gleefully exclaimed, "She's finished! She's cured!"

Harry looked at Adelyna. The brown slime was still everywhere. The diners were still frozen in resin. The cow dung smell permeated his skin. Harry felt sick. Harry retched and then yelled, "She's not cured! Everything is still gross!" Harry tried to hop toward the diner door in an effort to escape but slipped and slid in the slime.

Mr. Hedgehog, who was neither dismayed nor sickened by the situation, calmly said, "Harry, we must now effectuate the cure." Harry had no idea what "effectuate the cure" meant. But as Mr. Hedgehog came toward Harry, Harry started panicking. "Hold still, Harry, " said Mr. Hedgehog, who grabbed Harry around the waist and, to Harry's surprise, pinned Harry down on the diner countertop. Harry gasped for air. He began dreaming of swimming in his pond as he felt himself fainting.

While holding down Harry, Mr. Hedgehog grabbed Adelyna's arm and pulled her to Harry. "Kiss him! Now!" Mr. Hedgehog's tone was stern, commanding, and frankly, lacking in any patience whatsoever. He had grown weary of Adelyna's and Harry's ignorance. Their ignorance about dragon-flamed cooked hotdogs had led to the cow dung situation in the first place. Fairy village education was dramatically poor, thought Mr. Hedgehog.

Adelyna kissed Harry.

In Harry's fainting-dreamy state, he thought he felt a warm soft kiss on his cheek. Harry heard more dramatic yelling coming through his dreamy-fog. "Do it again!! Now!!! Now!! Now!"

Harry opened his eyes. He breathed. He was sitting on a counter stool, no longer pinned down by Mr. Hedgehog. Adelyna leaned forward and kissed Harry on the cheek. Harry felt an elation that he had never experienced, not even when he ate purple flies (which tasted like chocolate!). The kiss was warm and soft. Adelyna was smiling, her wings were fluttering, and a jasmine scent filled the air.

Everything had returned to normal. The diners were talking and eating again. The dragon chef was pouring sodas and scooping ice cream. The diner walls were shiny. The black and white tile floor sparkled. The jukebox was playing. The sun was streaming through the big picture windows.

"What a wonderful kiss!" exclaimed Harry, "Warm and soft and exactly like I dreamed about."
Adelyna smiled and gave Harry another warm soft kiss on his cheek. Then another.

"My work is done. Goodbye," said Mr. Hedgehog.

"Wait!" Harry jumped to Mr. Hedgehog. "Why didn't I become a prince when Adelyna gave me warm soft kisses?"

"I don't know," said Mr. Hedgehog. "Not all theories work out, Harry."

Harry sighed.

Adelyna frowned and said nothing.
Harry hopped back to the counter. He and Adelyna ate lunch— this time only fruit and ice cream. Thereafter, everyday for countless days, Harry and Adelyna ate lunch

and talked, and Harry received a warm soft kiss. Finally, after one hundred soft, warm kisses, Adelyna noticed two small, knobby bumps on Harry's back. "Those almost look like wing buds," she thought, but did not say anything to Harry for fear of disappointing him if they were not.

The next morning, Harry awoke to two large knobby bumps on his back. He was amazed. His first thought was to tell Adelyna, but he did not want to disappoint her if the knobs were not wing buds. What if he were sick? With frog bump disease? He hid in his pond while he pondered what to do.

By lunchtime, he felt two "pop-pops" on his back. The knobby bumps had sprouted into lustrous, mint green wings! Harry felt the happiest he had ever felt. He discovered immediately that flying was as easy as jumping. He flew to meet Adelyna at the diner. She was overjoyed. Harry would soon be her prince! Harry and Adelyna celebrated Harry's new wings with ice cream and soda. It was the best day ever!

Harry and Adelyna fluttered about the village spreading the good news that Harry was turning into Adelyna's prince. When they saw Mr. Hedgehog, they alighted at his feet. He said, "Ah! Good day Harry and my lovely fairy princess! I see Harry has wings. How delightful and exciting!"

"Yes. It most certainly is," said Adelyna in a royal business tone. She continued, "Harry and I have become the greatest of friends. We enjoy each other's company, we laugh, we sing, we talk, and now we fly together. But the reason I have been kissing frogs is because I'm looking for my fairy prince. When will Harry finish turning into a fairy prince?"

Harry had been wondering about this too but had been too shy and uncomfortable to bring up the issue with the princess. He was proud of his handsome wings and had the best fun flying. But Harry had begun to worry. Could he still swim in his pond if he had fairy prince legs and not frog legs?

Without hesitation, Mr. Hedgehog bluntly said, "Harry will never turn into a fairy prince. If Harry were going to become a fairy prince, he would have transformed immediately. Genetically speaking, some frogs, when kissed by a fairy princess, turn into fairy frogs not fairy princes. Harry is a fairy frog."

Both Harry's wings and the princess's wings spontaneously dropped and drooped at the unexpected news.

Mr. Hedgehog looked annoyed at the displays of emotion. The lack of education in these matters bothered him. "Listen," his tone was slightly condescending, but his words were positive, "Princess, it is obvious that you and Harry are meant to be friends and to enjoy glorious adventures together. Not every frog is a prince and not every prince is a frog. Not every princess kisses frogs and not every frog gets kissed by a princess. You two need to stop dreaming and just live. Go have fun!" Mr. Hedgehog lumbered away.

Based on Adelyna's frowning eyebrows and turned down lips, Harry could tell she was still grappling with their new reality. But Harry felt relieved. He felt liberated. There was no more pressure to become something he would never be or could be. There was no more pressure to fit into a role he could never fulfill. He was elated. He was more elated than he had ever been. He could fly and swim in his pond!

After Adelyna grew accustomed to their situation, she realized that the odds of kissing a frog and finding her prince were one in five hundred million. There were not five hundred million frogs in the fairy village. Adelyna stopped kissing frogs.

Harry and Adelyna continued their friendship. Everyday they flew and buzzed through the woods. Their daily adventures led to their rescue of fairy prince Roberto Goldfern, who was held captive by a troll.
After the rescue, Roberto moved into the fairy castle with Adelyna. They were married.

Subsequently, many baby fairies blossomed from goldenrod flowers and the village population increased exponentially. Adelyna established a Fairy Garden Village Town Council. She expanded the town's boundaries, erected a town fence, and hired a town staff.

Adelyna hired Mr. Hedgehog as the Chief of Village Emergency Management. His duties included daily instructional readings to the fairy children at the Fairy Village Library. These readings served as preventive emergency management by keeping ignorance at bay. Adelyna hired Harry as the Environmental Control Specialist responsible for monitoring pond water quality and general environmental conditions.

Harry liked his new job. In addition to Harry's home pond, four additional ponds were planned for the Village, plus a wishing well and a mermaid waterfall.

Harry soon found himself busy reviewing specifications and construction plans and obtaining the proper permits. He especially liked his mint green fairy wings because he could quickly fly from job site to job site.

Harry liked Adelyna and Roberto and the scads of dainty fairy babies, a few of whom he plucked from ponds from time to time when they lost control of their baby fluttering and flopped into the water. Although Harry liked purple flies and other tasty critters, Harry also liked diner food. Because Harry no longer had to kiss princesses, every now and then Harry treated himself to an amazing-tasting dragon-flame-cooked hotdog at the diner.

Most of all, Harry liked swimming in his pond with his fairy wings and frog legs. The experience was magnificent! Harry had never felt happier in his blue pond beside the fairy castle in a world hidden from humans.

Lauren Clemmons

Lois Thompson Bartholomew earned a BA in English from Brigham Young University and an MA in Publishing from Western Colorado University. A member of SCBWI and TAF, her YA novel The White Dove was published by Houghton Mifflin and republished by PennCreekPress. She is a lover of reading, writing, and books,

The Visitor

At 4 AM
While you were sleeping,
The moon stopped by to visit.
Full and round,
He peeked through
The bare branches
Of the neighbor's oak tree,
And smiled down
Into our garden.

-2-
Our golden fence of blooming forsythia
Reached up her arms
To catch him.
But he couldn't stay
While you were sleeping
At 4 AM.

Lois Thompson Bartholomew

Jesse McCorvey is a freelancer who has written numerous pieces throughout his career, mostly short stories and poems, and a few songs along the way. This is the beginning of his first novel about a widowed woman's strength, hardened by rebellion and unexpected life situations, and the spectacular legacy she creates.

First Chapter

"Well, he was dead to me anyway."
It was a comment more suited to a Mafia movie, and yet it came from a wife who was just notified of her husband's death in a car accident. But the Mafia reference was not very far off.

Barbara Holden was cold and stoic as she responded to the two State Patrol officers at her front door. They were there to announce her husband's death earlier that night.
"Mrs. Holden, we are sorry to inform you that your husband, Ron Holden, was killed in a car accident earlier this evening."

Her initial, blunt comment was a little surprising to the officers, their eyes widened as they glared at each other. They had seen and heard nearly everything in these situations. And, they also knew that initial, indifferent reactions are often followed by more serious, emotional outbursts. Barb could only look down and shake her head.

She lived alone, they had been separated for years. Ron
had been at a Super Bowl party with his 'seedy business
buddies' and called her earlier from the club. Ron, a
chronic gambler who would often bet upwards of $100,000,
bragged on their earlier phone call that he won over
$250,000 on the game. It was the largest amount she had
ever heard him talk about in a gambling win. And, he
mentioned that he had it all in a briefcase – in cash. She
could only shake her head even more.

"What an idiot," she murmured out loud. The Officers
heard it and their eyes opened a little wider.
Then her thoughts were too risky to verbalize: "What an
absolute idiot," she mused. "Driving by himself, after
partying all night, with a quarter of a million dollars in the
seat next to him. And knowing his "silent partners" were
upset that he beat them out of their cash."

Her anger came out as sarcasm as she spoke to the
policemen, "Well, did he have a 'blonde bombshell' with
him? You said it was an 'accident'; are you sure about
that? Did his car blow up? Did somebody run them off the
road?"

Again, the two officers glanced eye to eye; they couldn't
answer. It was too much for them to process. The air was
heavy and still for a moment. Barb's phone broke the
silence and she walked to the kitchen to answer it. It was
her oldest son, Allen, who worked side by side with his
Dad.

"Mom, I've got some bad news. Some really bad news, and I wish I was there to tell you personally. Dad's - dead. He died in a car accident about an hour ago. We are going to deal with this and get through it, Mom, I promise. I've called Carol and Lynn and they are heading to your place right now. I'm coming over too, but I have to go to Dad's house first. Before the Police get there."

"Wait, Allen, the Police are here now, at my place," she whispered. "How do you know about this already? They're just telling me now. Did they notify you first?"

"They're at your house now?" he said. "Are they already investigating? Did they find Dad's stuff from the car?"

"Allen, what are you talking about? Investigating what – what stuff? What in the hell have you been up to? Get your ass over here right now and tell me what's going on." Her voice was escalating louder as the anger was boiling over.

The officers walked into the kitchen to interrupt. "Uh, Mrs. Holden, Mrs. Holden, are you okay?"

"Yes, yes, I'm fine. It's my son. He's upset. I'm sure you can understand." She held her hand over the phone so Allen couldn't hear. "Let me calm him down and tell him to come over here."
"We would be glad to get him if you think that is best. Hate to have another accident tonight with someone who shouldn't be driving."

"No, no, I think he will be okay. I'll have my sister go and pick him up. Just give me a moment."

She turned away to speak very directly into the phone, but louder, fully realizing she would be easily heard. "Allen, get hold of yourself and come on over. Call Carol to pick you up. Get over here and we will get through this. The Police are over here and they need to talk to me. Okay, goodbye."

"Well, uh, we are still investigating, Mrs. Holden. We we will let you know as soon as possible about our determination. One thing we will need very soon; the body has to be identified by a family member; you can send someone else if you wish."

"I've got family coming over; I may get one of them to do it." As she spoke, she started thinking about family, her Italian heritage. How their family history was so broken with tragic deaths like this. How the men of her family get involved in the most dangerous of businesses. And, how the women are left to handle things after they're gone.

"Can we wait here with you until they arrive? We'd rather not leave you here alone, if you don't mind."

Awakened back to reality by their comments, she shook her head to focus. "What did you say; you're worried about me being alone? Hell, I live my entire shitty life alone. Nobody else worries about me being alone. Certainly not

84

my HUSBAND." She paused for a moment, realizing she had gone too far. "I'm sorry, forgive me. No, no, you don't have to worry, they'll be here in a minute. You can go and do whatever else you have to do. I'll be fine. Thanks for the concern."

"We have his personal belongings from his car. We collected them at the hospital and we have them in a box in our Patrol Car. All of his jewelry, his wallet, and everything in his pockets are in a plastic bag. There was also a briefcase and it is there as well." They paused as they spoke.

"His briefcase was locked. We could have broken into it, but, we thought tonight had enough drama and tragedy. It's part of his personal property, and you can have it all." We are not going to pursue anything more."

They brought everything in and gave it to Barb. She tried NOT to look hard at the briefcase, and simply took it all in a bundle from the officers. "I will deal with all this later. You don't have to stay, I'll be fine."

She closed the door to silence, but her mind was racing. She felt numb, then shook her head in devastation. The shock and anger were married in her thoughts as she tried to center herself on the reality of what happened. Then the disbelief would quickly surface, but fade just as fast.

The shock and surprise were fading also, which left anger to multiply. And that anger would be her motivator, the

driving force to her future. But she just could not
comprehend that she was in this situation.

"No, wait, I've known this was coming for years," she
blurted out loud. "He's lucky he lived this long. Those
assholes he hung around with were horrible. His entire,
sordid life was horrible. And, he made my life horrible.
Now, my son is involved in it too."

There were no tears, no sadness, no sorrow – only anger, to
the nth degree. She thought about Ron, dead on a slab in
the morgue. "What a horrible scene," she thought. And yet
she couldn't get past 'angry'. Instead, she started thinking
about how to use this calamity to "put some sense" into her
son Allen. Maybe he should go identify the body. He was
obviously entangled in Ron's seedy business more than she
realized. Maybe, just maybe, if he saw how horrible things
can end up in Ron's crazy world, he would think about
getting a real job. One that didn't interact with the worst
people imaginable. "Maybe looking down on his father in
the morgue will shake him out of this."

"So this is how it ends," she thought. "Our family
destroyed by an absolute senseless lifestyle.

Living the last parts of my life by myself, without a job, or
support from anybody. And I am still alone. More alone
than I have ever been."

But Barb Holden was a fighter. She came from a long line
of fighters. Her Italian mother and grandmother fought

hard to keep their families together throughout a storied
and tumultuous era in South Chicago.

She was strong. Enduring and persevering through life
with Ron only increased her strength. She was tough.
Hardened by years of being married to a man nobody could
live with. But mostly, she was a survivor. Inheriting
strength from the women before her, and building
toughness through just living her life. Living life with Ron.

But that was over, his life was over. And her life had just
begun a new chapter – a chapter of strength. Strength she
would need to overcome some of the disastrous decisions
Ron had made. Decisions that would change the course of
her life forever.

Jesse McCorvey

Anne Glasser Brennan is an inspirational essayist, retreat leader and speaker from Cary, North Carolina. Her first book, God Does Not Take Naps, A Collection of Inspirational Essays, Poems and Reflections is readying for publication. Anne is a Pastoral Care Ministry volunteer and aspires to be a hospice chaplain.

God is The Author of My Day

God is The Author.

Mother's Day, when you are not a mother, is hard. I wish more than anything that I was a mother, but I am not. I am grateful that I had a wonderful mother. She was the sunshine of my life and I tell her that every time I get the chance. Hopefully, your Mom is alive and well, but if not, she is in Heaven with the angels, and as my father would say, "enjoying the Beatific Vision." Close in proximity or up above, Moms are forever in our hearts.

Being overly self-absorbed, I wished Mother's Day would pass quickly. I sat in my little writing room staring at a blank screen. Turning toward a window, I gazed at a photo of my brother and sister-in-law on their wedding day in 2001. They exuded radiance and joy. What a happy time, a happy chapter, a happy couple. Nine years later, following their tragic deaths in an accident, Larkin Funeral Home placed the same wedding photo on the In Loving Memory card. Joe and Kelly are remembered for the lifetime of precious memories we shared.

Would that I could rewrite the chapter and bring them back. But I can't because…

God is The Author.
The title was reinforced this week when I attended a graduation ceremony at the Governor Morehead School in Raleigh, North Carolina. Founded in 1845, it is the eighth-oldest school for the blind in the country. Through my work at the nonprofit Triangle Radio Reading Service and the development of a program for blind and vision impaired teens in radio broadcasting called T3 Teens Tools Talent, I got to know GMS students with delightful personalities, varying aspirations, and a range of low vision or partial sight to those who are totally blind meaning no light perception. Four of the graduates on the stage were totally blind.

The Commencement Speaker, a seasoned and effective Orientation and Mobility Specialist, knew each graduate personally, as he taught them O&M. He shared inspirational stories and funny stories about each student, and it was clear that he had learned as much from their drive and determination as they had learned from him. It was an excellent keynote.

Blindness empowered and inspired great resilience in these graduates to overcome obstacles that most teenagers would never have to consider, such as relying on an Orientation &

Mobility Specialist to teach them how to travel the school campus safely with little or no sight.

The most outstanding speaker, however, the most memorable speaker that morning was Brandon. He walked with assistance to the podium and said, "Welcome everyone to Commencement 2016." And then it was silent. The silence lasted what seemed a long time. Brandon's Mom left the audience to approach the podium, stayed a minute or so before returning to her seat. Brandon again welcomed everyone. And again, the welcome was followed by silence. At first, I thought that it might be stage fright, but that was not the case.

 Brandon finally began his speech, speaking slowly and tentatively. With humor and quiet dignity, he shared that life had been "going along pretty well." He achieved good grades on the A-B Honor Roll in middle school. His dream "was to become a doctor." Then, one day, Brandon and his parents learned that he had a brain tumor. I don't know how old he was, but he was old enough to be told that the surgery could impact his sight, his mobility, and his intelligence. Brandon was told he had to make a choice. He chose to keep his intelligence.

Can you imagine being twelve or thirteen years old and telling a doctor that you want to keep your intelligence while possibly or probably losing your sight and mobility? I can't imagine, and yet, listening to Brandon, I could imagine the devastating options. Brandon is blind, he has mobility challenges, and, yes, he has cognitive challenges

with short-term memory. Meanwhile, despite his
challenges, Brandon was the Salutatorian.

Everyone in that auditorium was profoundly moved by the
content and delivery of an incredible speech. His devoted
Mom in the background helped him with what may have
been a copy of the speech he had written on her I-phone.
Expressing his heartfelt gratitude to the teachers, the
school, and his peers, Brandon received a standing ovation.
No surprise. It is something that I will never forget. There
wasn't a dry eye in the house.

God is The Author.
God knows everything about us. Those of us who are
"cradle Catholics" believe that God knows "how many
hairs there are (or were!) on your head." Luke 12:7 Yea,
the very hairs of your head are all numbered. He knows
what the day is going to bring, including natural disasters
like tornadoes and hurricanes and natural delights like
weddings and new babies. He knows of our feelings, our
dreams, our quirks, our failures, our longings, and our
needs.

God hopes that each one of us will be like Brandon.

God wants us to make tough choices and live with humility
during difficult times. He wants us to grow and become
more compassionate and caring because of tough times. He
wants us to live faithfully. He also wants us to know that
we are never alone. We walk by faith and not by sight
because He is ever at our sides.

God gives us situations, "chapters" that we wish He would change, edit, or completely rewrite.
How often have you thought to yourself or looked heavenward and said, "OK, God, I really need a break," or "OK, Dear Lord, I am at my absolute wit's end, please cut me some slack."

You can be sure He hears our pleas, prayers, and petitions, every single one. However, changing, editing, or completely rewriting the book of life that has our names on it is not His plan.

Our work in today's chapter is to trust that God is constantly beside us. If we truly believe that (it's called faith), He grants us grace to accept the things that we cannot change. He grants us the grace to plod on through the toughest of times knowing that the sun will come out tomorrow and peaceful waters are where He is leading us even if it seems the total opposite.

No one said that it was going to be easy. But God told you, and He continues to tell you second by second that you are His precious child, His beautiful creation, His miracle, just like Brandon.

God is The Author of my day. He is The Author of all our days.

Make this chapter the best it can be. You can do it! Remember, there are no rewrites. I have faith in you! More importantly, God has faith in you, too!

The Time Stamp

The timestamp has many uses and connotations. Some uses are surprises, some are tedious, some are funny, even belly-busters, and there is an ultra-important use not to be taken lightly; it is the timestamp that no one can avoid. It does not have a happy connotation. But it does have an optimistic use!

Let's start with the surprise timestamp. A school tax bill marked "Paid in Full" with a timestamp of January 30, 2024, came in the mail for my parent's house which was sold nine months ago. It was good news because the document had a second timestamped Paid in Full for the previous year when my father paid the bill. The double timestamped document was a surprise!

Receiving the School Tax Notice gave me pause to reflect on the outstanding education my brothers, Chris and Joe, and I were afforded by the Burnt Hills-Ballston Lake Central School system in upstate New York. We three graduated from BH-BL Senior High School with Regents Diplomas in the 1970s. We were well-prepared for our respective next steps thanks to great teachers like Mrs. Christie. Her tedious timed typing tests followed by timestamps may have had something to do with our future paths, mine especially since I am typing all the time!

The tedious timestamp explanation goes back fifty years to ninth grade when Mrs. Christie gave 10-minute timed typing tests every Thursday once everyone achieved eye-hand coordination sufficient to employ ASDF JKL; (the home row on the keyboard and the first thing taught back then in typing class). We were NOT allowed to look at our hands while typing from the script. No exceptions. We used manual typewriters. Correct keys were nonexistent. Does anyone remember a carriage return? Well, Mrs. Christie would catch you if you were thinking about looking at your hands! She had eyes behind her head and a serious sixth sense! My classmates and I strove for a 100%-timestamp at the close of the timed and very tedious typing tests.

From tedium to hilarity, we now discuss the funny use of the timestamp. I moved to North Carolina twenty years after high school graduation. From my home in Cary, there were numerous visits back to the family homestead, becoming more frequent and longer in duration as my parents aged. Role reversal happened, and caretaking became my role. I wouldn't trade a single minute or precious memory, some of them hysterical. In the final stretch, the last five-year period, I never failed to check the timestamps, also known as expiration dates, on all the condiments in the refrigerator and cabinets, medicines, cereal, and canned goods.

Enter Mrs. Nosypants. She/ I took over with zeal while ruthlessly tossing refrigerated products that had long since been edible. My parents would assure me that they had cast-iron stomachs, and their advancing age was a testament to their more than satisfactory digestion! How often we disagreed and rolled our eyes collectively about me disposing of their larder! They would succumb, sometimes grudgingly, and then we laughed. My dear husband Ed would then take me to Price Chopper, where I purchased replacements for everything to ensure fewer GERD attacks. (If you are old, you know what GERD is because you have it. If you are young, it's Gastric Esophageal Reflux Disease. If you live long enough, you will eventually get it if you like to eat anything you shouldn't eat or drink and in small or copious quantities.). Timestamps, in the case of food, are there for a reason! Ha!

The final use of the timestamp is unavoidable and daunting. However, if you believe in Heaven, and I do, the final timestamp marks the beginning of something new, beautiful, and forever.

My brother Chris and I kept vigil in a hospital room with our beloved father a little over one year ago. Surrounded by caring, competent, and compassionate doctors, nurses, aides, and, well, everyone we encountered it seemed, Pop's former family practice doctor came to see him and brought comfort to us all while we waited, watched, and companioned him on his final earthly journey. Pop slept peacefully during John's visit, hearing the gentle tones, if not the content of our voices. We spoke about the circle of life. John and our brother Joe were high school classmates.

Pop had not seen John in years, but he always spoke of him with great fondness. The feelings were clearly mutual. The time bedside, holding Pop's hands, was tender, especially when John shared with me his mother-in-law's passing several months before. A great lady, like my folks, all from

The Greatest Generation, she told him before her journey to
Heaven, "You know, John, we all have a timestamp."
We all have a timestamp. That exchange struck me, and it
stuck with me. It reminded me that God is the author of my
day and yours, too. Our days are numbered.

Psalm 139:16 "You saw me before I was born. The days
allotted to me had all been recorded in your book, before
any of them ever began."

Until we reach our timestamp, or our timestamp reaches us,
each day God grants is a gift. Each day God entrusts us
with a purpose to His service. We need only to be open and
to trust.

Psalm 138:8 "The Lord will fulfill his purpose for me; your
steadfast love, O Lord, endures forever."

We believe that we are indestructible and that we'll live
forever when we are young. Retirement age creeps up and
octogenarians-plus we become if we are lucky! Inevitably,
something happens, and we change our indestructible tune,
realize our mortality, and turn to God.

Following a colon cancer diagnosis received during
COVID, and yes, with a grin that came right through the
email, our dear friend Ron wrote: "Well, folks, one thing is
for sure, not one of us is getting out of this life alive." How
true for this world, not so for eternity.
Jesus tells us differently.

John 10:28 "I give them eternal life, and they shall never perish."

Yes, the timestamp has many uses and connotations. Some are surprises, some are tedious, some are funny, and only one is forever.

May you use the time you are given on this planet
To be a blessing to others
In His Holy Name.

May you trust in God
In all His ways
All your days

May you seek
To be entrusted with God's special purpose
for you today.
And with His abiding grace, act faithfully on it

May you find eternal life
Someday
When your timestamp is called.
Amen

Anne Glasser Brennan

Erika Hoffman taught high school, raised her four children, and now writes non-fiction narratives, travel articles and educational pieces. Her books are collections of her published stories and personal essays.

Beautiful Teeth at the Moulin Rouge

"Paris is always a good idea," Audrey Hepburn once famously declared. Before I ventured off leaving Raleigh-Durham Airport for Charles De Gaulle Airport on October 25, 2023, I heard the following warnings from sundry folks: "Bedbugs found at the Parisian hotels now;" " The subways are unsafe and bedbugs there too;" "The streets stay filthy, and Paris stinks;" "Every week, yellow vests are protesting something and on strike;" "Watch out for pickpockets, especially in museums and touristy places."

"Parisians don't like Americans and will treat you rudely;" "With all that is going on in the world now, aren't you worried about the Muslim population in France?" Finally, these Debbie Downers concluded, "Paris is so expensive!"

I packed Vick's Vapor Rub because I did research on You Tube and saw that this old remedy combats bedbugs. I wore a passport/wallet/pocket combo around my neck. My footwear — trusty old sneakers that have traipsed through all sorts of stuff and wouldn't fall victim to cobblestones as tripping hazards. I've suffered snobs before. Hey, is the

City of Light more expensive than NYC? Are their subways more dangerous than ours in the Big Apple?

And so, I went! The flight was delightful. I didn't have anyone the size of the Jolly Green Giant seated next to me and lopping over. The hotel had no bedbugs. The staff were accommodating and friendly. Except for dog poop from pedigree, posh, frou-frou canines, the streets were immaculate. No one was protesting anything, anywhere. Handsome gendarmes and adorable female police with guns were stationed around sites like Notre Dame. I didn't see gypsies. I didn't get pickpocketed or harassed or even approached by any unsavory character. Unlike other times I've been to Paris in 1961, 1968, 1971, 1981, 1992, the Parisians weren't haughty, rude, unpleasant, or pretentious. They were as nice as North Carolinian folks, and the city was not as expensive as Westchester County, New York. The Metro was clean and safe. A lot of stairs, though!

Did I visit the Eiffel Tower? No! Been there done that. I enjoyed seeing it glitter and fascinate from afar; at night, it's lit up and sparkles. I never realized before how much the Eiffel Tower looks like a bridge on its side until a guide pointed that out. Did I visit Notre Dame Cathedral in Paris? Yes and no. I've been inside before, of course. Now they are refurbishing it after the catastrophic fire, trying to restore it before the Olympic Games this summer 2024. Huge placards with photos of the inferno revealed what it looked like immediately after the fire. Also, these photos showed the cleaning process of the sooty statues within. Did I visit Montmartre where the artists hang out?

Did I enter the dazzling white Sacre Coeur Church atop the mountains of stairs? Sure, but we took a trolley up. Stairs are for teens and sadists. It's much more crowded now than decades ago, and many of the artists who sketch your likeness are Chinese.

What did I do differently from my other trips? For starters, I went to the catacombs. Sometimes, Paris is called Lutece because Romans in the third century before Christ named it after the swampy, muddy area around the Seine River. The beautiful limestone buildings like Notre Dame came from rock quarried below the city. Paris is riddled with ancient quarries. In the 18th century, houses caved in and tumbled into these cavities beneath Paris. In 1786, they began filling up this network of gypsum and chalk quarries with bones from cemeteries. Skulls and femurs form bone walls in the ossuary below Paris. The catacombs are a memorial to those who lived and died in the City of Light from the 14th to the 18th century. Famous bones rest there too, like Moliere's and those of the sister of Louis the 16th. I didn't want to add to this collection and worried about doing just that when I read ahead of time that there were 132 spiral steps down,112 back up, no lavatories, and six miles of claustrophobia-causing tunnels that are lined with countless bones. No one with a heart condition should try it, warned the guidebooks. My nerves weren't calmed either when I turned to my husband before entering and asked, "I'm not as young as I look. You think I can do this?" and he answered, "I'm not carrying you back up."

They allow folks down—only a certain number of people—
every fifteen minutes. You must reserve your place a week
ahead but no earlier than a week before. As we marched
along, it didn't help my mental state when an American
family came up behind us, and the 11-year-old girl
continuously shrieked: "Mommy, we're going to die down
here!" I plastered myself along the narrow walls being
careful not to dislodge any antique bones or hollowed out
eye socket skulls so that the unsettling family could
squeeze by.

Grisly. Yes. Macabre. Definitely. Halloween was
approaching. It's not a holiday they much practice in
France, which is surprising, when you visit this site. They
say the remains of six million people are housed down
there. It all began because the cemeteries housed bodies in
unsanitary ways causing the city to smell. Clearing these
churchyards also gave more land to the living. And it
provided a purpose for the huge underground labyrinth of
corridors, caused by mining, which lay below the city. The
bones have commemorative slabs engraved with the origin
of the remains, and the year they were transferred to the
catacombs. As you walk along there are "comforting
messages" engraved such as: "If perchance you have seen
men die, know that the same fate awaits you." Sometimes,
it's better not to be able to translate French!

When my husband and I finally emerged after spying a
huge sink hole overhead, I suggested we see something a
little more uplifting. We crossed the street and descended
underground again to the Metro to carry us to the Cite to

see Sainte Chapelle, which has the most beautiful stained-glass windows in the world.

Speaking of beautiful, that night we taxied over to the Moulin Rouge and saw the most extravagantly perfect female bodies wearing only the skimpiest thongs ever created. They danced, strutted, and performed gymnastic contortions I'd not thought humanly possible. On route back to the hotel, I said to my husband Byron and our other companions in the cab. "Those girls had the most beautiful teeth I've ever seen."
"And they were only a cup A or B," Peggy said.

"TEETH!" I emphasized. I reiterated, "Teeth" and pointed to my mouth.
 "Oh, I thought you said t…"
 "I know what you thought I said!"
 We laughed.

Paris is always a good idea.

Erika Hoffman

Terri DeGezelle Michels is author and photographer, has published 64 children's non-fiction books, as well as more than 100 magazine articles, and a fiction picture book, Simon of Cyrene, Legend of the Easter Egg. Terri shares her art and writing experiences during school visits where she encourages students to follow their dreams.

Know But to God

The Procession to the Tomb of the Unknown

November 11, 1921, an armistice declared,
Ended the war to end all wars.
Americans pause to remember those who paid the supreme price.
Bring home one of our own, the public cried, "An unknown for all to honor, to rest at Arlington National Cemetery."
These words seal the coffin: "An unknown soldier who gave his life in the Great War."
Rain-soaked flag-draped coffin laid in state for 48 solemn hours.
Thousands of people, young and old, from near and far
All came to pay honor and their last respects.
Under a gray, sodden sky, six matching horses pull the caisson.
Two columns of body bearers take their places.
And the parade begins.
Major General Ernest Bandholtz leads the parade.
Five clergy carrying their Bibles follow behind.

President Harding, his Army Chief of Staff, Vice President,
Chief of Naval Operations, Chief Justice of the United
States, and the Commandant of the Coast Guard march in
support of one of their fallen troopers.
The Army Drum Corps beating out the quick-time cadence
follow behind.
And the parade marches on.

A small group of most courageous sons, the Medal of
Honor heroes,
Eight abreast some old and frail, others young and erect,
supporting one another.
Generals, admirals, and troops representing every military
branch fall into formation.
Each thinking the Unknown could have been me.
And the parade marches on.

Kings, dignitaries, and diplomats from far and wide join the
parade.
The Supreme Court judges form a single line.
Cabinet members span five abreast,
And the parade marches on.

Governors, senators, and congressmen join side-by-side.
In a sea of black and gray, a splash of snow-white shines
forth.
Oklahoma Representative, Miss Alice Robertson, wears her
Red Cross uniform proudly.
And the parade marches on.
Veterans from every state, marching once more in uniform,
Accompanying a fellow comrade to his final resting place.

Bringing up the rear: former President and Mrs. Woodrow
Wilson.
And the parade marches on.

At the gates of Arlington National Cemetery, a Marine
Band takes over.
The steady beat of a funeral march keeps time.
After many invocations, with final words freshly spoken,
Washington D.C.'s noontime bells ring forth.
For two minutes of scared silence, the country pauses and
prays.
The choir sings, "America."
President Harding speaks: "We don't know…of his birth,
But we do know of the glory of his death.
He died with faith in his heart and hope on his lips."

Two grieving mothers, one American and the other British,
Lay wreaths honoring all mothers who have lost a child.
Lastly, Chief Plenty Coos, calls on the Great Spirit with
tribal chant.
Placed upon the coffin is his war club and war bonnet, he
declares, "I hope …there will be peace to all men
hereafter."
Sprinkled in the grave, two inches of soil from battlefields
of France, cushioning the eternal rest of the Unknown.
Taps sound their good night and good rest wishes for the
Unknown,
Cannons sound a 21-gun salute.
 He is home, the Unknown, to sleep forever among his own.
Terri DeGezelle Michels

Margaret Toman vigils in front of Central Prison every Monday, advocating against the death penalty. Retired, she is a former long-term caregiver who writes memoir, letters to the editor, Op Eds and participates in discussion groups about current affairs. She relishes classical music, asparagus and mischievous Whiskey sours.

Ode to a Sea Creature

Last week, for my 76th birthday, after years of declaring that I would not be caught dead in a bathing suit, I bought one. I had cornered myself into it by signing up for a free aquatic aerobics class at the Wellness Center. The next day, for the first time in probably 45 years, I stepped into a swimming pool. Forty years ago, I was bikini-fit and proud. This time, my older, plumper self-cringed from the eyes of others as I walked out onto the pool deck, jumped in and immersed. The water embraced me warmly, forgiving my folds and flaws, swirling around my body like the hands of an eager lover. I submerged myself up to my neck and wondered how I could have forsaken something so pleasantly sensual for so long.

Distanced around me in the pool were 16 other women of a certain age, all of us on a quest to forestall time and to preserve the vestiges of youth and beauty. A few warm smiles dotted the group; most appeared to be measuring and comparing, in the secretly competitive way some do even when there no men present. On the pool deck, a slim young woman pressed a button. "Are you ready?" she asked, as "Fe-fe fi-fi fo-fo fum" revved up. I wondered briefly if the devil with the blue dress on, ever swam in it.

"Run" the young woman commanded – "that way", a finger pointed to the right. I struggled to run against the water's unyielding resistance. "Now the other way!" I complied as best I could. "Now march in place, raise your knees high – one, two, three, four…Use your arms!" My heart pounded, my lungs heaved, my limbs and shoulders jived to the music, catching the beat, splashing exuberantly. I was beginning to get the hang of it. I felt like the devil with the blue suit on.

"Now hop", came the order. "Hop-hop-hop-hop… Now bring both knees up when you hop" she yelled. That is not easy the first few times you try it. I launched myself up, raising both knees, only to fall to one side or the other on the way down, like a breaching whale with a balance problem. I felt clumsy and graceless. And then, like a key that finds the right lock, I began to laugh, out loud, uncontrollably, uproariously, at myself. I could not stop. The thumping music and splashing drowned out the sound of my laughter for most participants but the woman to my right gave me a stare that reflected how deranged she suspected I might be. I didn't care; I continued hopping, splashing and laughing, gasping for breath. In that laughter was release, relief, acceptance, wildness, wholeness and freedom. I may have looked ridiculous, but I was having fun, a dimension of life I want to explore more often this year.

After 45 minutes of running, marching and hopping the music ended and the ladies and I climbed breathless from the pool, revealing time's vandalisms -- love handles, scars from surgeries or accidents or childbirth, stretch marks, birth marks, skin discolorations, wrinkles, balding heads, pooched tummies, odd moles, puffy thighs, a missing breast. Life, lived. The woman who had been next to me stared intently as I left the pool deck. I imagined her describing to her friends the hysterical fool in the pool, although by then I really didn't care. Buying that bathing suit, which I could not afford and which, even as I bought it swore I would never be seen in, was an act of defiance against insecurities too long unconfronted.

In the locker room a rotund woman, dripping wet in a suit that was working hard to cover everything, walked over amiably and welcomed me to the class. She could have been a sea creature. Long soggy tentacles of hair hung from a nearly bald scalp; her face was as wrinkled and reddened as brain coral. Across an expanse of upper arm fanned a once colorful tattoo. Her broad smile revealed long neglected teeth. She said she had seen me struggling and laughing in the water, admired my spunk, thought I had the right attitude. "You're a lot nicer than most of the old witches around here" she whispered conspiratorially. "I hope you come back." About her was not a trace of self-consciousness or fear of what my reaction to her appearance might be. She was a role model of great beauty.

"Yes", I smiled. "I will come back."

Margaritaville

It is late Saturday night and I am perched on the third barstool from the left at The Locked and Loaded Grill. Outside are Harley "Boss Hogs" detailed to a spotless sheen by their proud owners. Inside, Band 454 is rocking the walls.

I am not a biker. I am a 77 year old single woman with graying hair wearing a pearl necklace and earrings who drives a Toyota Corolla and prefers classical music, and I'm out on my own for the evening. Curious glances when I walk into Locked and Loaded do not bother me nor do I let what are likely opposing opinions regarding gun

control stop me. Just this morning I rallied with the
"March for Our Lives" gun control crowd at the legislative
building. I am not here in my role as public advocate but as
private supplicant, asking the edgy, counter culture
atmosphere to distract me from concerns about this moment
in history.

In the 4-1/2 hours I have been sitting on this stool, I
have devoured a healthy meal, nursed two crisp-clean beers
and chatted with friendly bartenders in the rare moments
they weren't filling drink orders. Mostly, I sit quietly and
watch steel wool women with deep cleavage and strategic
tattoos flirt like wild birds with cocky men wearing silver
chains and black Harley vests. Their arms display full
sleeve body art. It is Saturday Night Live in the biker bar;
every seat and stool is filled; the bartenders scramble to
keep up. Drinks pour continuously. The band sustains a
hard, deafening beat. Meet ups, hook ups, flirtations, and
cycle talk are everywhere. So is braggadocio, interspersed
with raucous laughter.

When the men lean across the bar from behind me
to order a drink or pay a bill, they smell of whiskey and
strong cologne. Their smiles are friendly when they
apologize for reaching around me. They politely call me
"ma'am", which reminds me how old I am in this place.
As the night goes on, the atmosphere changes in a
predictable pattern several times until, around the 3rd hour
of imbibing, inhibitions disappear and what was previously
flirtatious turns openly sensual. Bartenders call this
phenomena "bar weather" and it is as predictable and as
reassuring as the turning of the seasons. Until it isn't.

To the left from where I sit at the bar is a long
hallway which passes a small coffee closet, two pool tables,
the restrooms and at the far end, the door to the kitchen. It
was around 11:30 when odd movements in the hall caught
my attention. Two men, one tall and bald, one short with
thick hair, were proceeding in my direction exchanging

what appeared at first to be mock punches. As they got closer the punches escalated into hot, furious battle. They tangled and cursed and fell down on the floor together, arms and legs flailing, punches hammering back and forth. The tall man's head struck the doorjamb of the coffee closet on the way down. Blood poured. As if orchestrated for a movie set, bartenders and patrons rushed to intercede, piled on. Shouting ensued, cell phones lit up with calls to 911. I found my sedate, pearl earringed self sitting on a barstool just a few feet away from a full fledged bar room brawl that I watched while sipping the last of my beer. My initial instinct was to do something helpful. I curbed it. I had no idea what, if anything, I could do so I watched with what now strikes me as an eerie calm and did nothing. It was, in retrospect, a wise decision given the furiously battling maze of male arms, legs, and bodies. The band, meanwhile, who saw it all, wisely or humorously or perhaps both, continued their rollicking rendition of "I Love Rock and Roll".

Police appeared and hauled the two hot heads out of the bar, still flailing, leaving behind a floor slick with blood. Like everyone else I wanted to know what real or imagined transgression had precipitated the fight. I knew that both men had been drinking for a while. Earlier in the evening, the tall, bald, man and his date had beguiled each other for hours on the other side of the bar from me, besotted in more ways than one. They had moved to the stage area and apparently, he had casually draped his arm around the shorter man's girlfriend, sparking a jealous rage. It was after midnight when I got home. The distraction I sought from the Locked and Loaded Grill was achieved more effectively than I could have imagined. It occurs to me that I should be more distressed by the violence. Certainly, I hope the two men are okay and I am vastly relieved that fists flew rather than bullets. I will double down on my efforts for sensible gun control. But I have to

admit that on arriving home I looked in the mirror at an
aging woman with graying hair, wearing pearl earrings and
saw her laughing a little. I laughed back.
It was just another night in Margaritaville.

Margaret Toman

Tom Harmon lives with his wife in Ontario, Canada, an ex-pat from Florida. He writes informed by constant scenery changes as a child and an adult. A horror and science fiction writer that uses the spectrum of human emotion and uncertainty of new science to relate a lingering sense of dread people feel in new landscapes; emotional and physical.

Chapter 6 from Obscura
Thread

The approach of the next room became a foreboding consternation that made Elias' skin run cold. An involuntary choke strangled his throat when he even considered what lay ahead; bringing himself to approach another one of these rooms was becoming as grim a thought as not making it out at all. A constant silent ringing in his ears bore a hole through his thoughts; the dimming light gave way to more anxiety, which shattered any gathered calm he had accumulated.

The weight, the crushing weight, kept piling a tremendous agonizing vice grip on his nerves. A bleak, dusty fog acted in a manner that more resembled a metastasis within a human body, eventually engulfing the entirety of the containers like spreading cancer. Damp wooden floors and steel walls encased Elias, who had become the parasite in this lengthy host's body; each trap felt more like the immune system trying harder to eradicate the unfortunate intruder. An expertly designed course awaited him, but he knew he needed to gain a bit of resolve after this latest mental grinding trap.

"What the fuck could this even consist of? I can't handle too much more of this."

Jagged rusty holes where the twisted wires crept inside this dungeon kept reminding him that there was an outside— even if he had no idea what was on the other side. The flashlight acted as a fading beacon of hope and a sort of timer which Elias needed to keep in mind, or he was going to have to traverse these terrors in pitch-black darkness, forever altering the playing field and contorting this horrible maze-like configuration out of his favor.

"I have to keep going...."

"This is only as fucked up as I let myself believe it is"—a thought that was poured into the mind of the abused to excuse and accept the horrific and pernicious situation that anyone in his predicament faced. Elias knew by the cracked molars and jagged incisors that crudely protruded from parts of his swollen gum line that he no longer had the same appearance he once did. There was no mirror needed to deduce that fact. Vanity was the last thing on his mind, but it was a factor nonetheless. If the crisis he faced ended now, he would still be leaving this human cage as someone almost wholly unrecognizable.

When he refocused his attention, what was instantly recognizable—standing ready and waiting— was the next wall in front of him. A gray, tall, perfectly cut and shaped rectangular barrier once again blocked the view of his destination. This was the most egregious, consistent torture above all others, ailing Elias. He could take everything else, but these damn walls were starting to brew and bubble his ire. These fucking walls were a constant slap in his already injured mouth, a sizable and chunky spit in the face that kept happening over and over. This was the monotonous drip on his forehead that was pushing him a bit further from the sane mental plane, the overwhelming chaos that impeded his progression forward intentionally to make him formulate a plan— or whatever this piece of shit had intended. Elias was over it all, and nothing could melt this jumbled amalgam of boisterous annoyance and burning need for vengeance against this unseen monster who made the worst mistake of his short life by selecting to trap him like an animal.

The silence was deafening, and the throbbing of a low tone made of nothingness was delivered to the malleus and on to the incus, then finally to the stapes to bring forth a large batch of quiet so thick it could have its own physical form.

The ears functioned perfectly and in brilliant synchronicity, but it seemed they now manufactured only faint clicks in a settling chamber made of steel and wood. All vague translations of ticks and slight adjusting boards or metal framing now swirled in his cochlea, churning slight

reverberations into the distant cadence of this massive
tunnel's voice.

Elias started to miss that god-awful shrieking moment
before; at least, it was recognizable chaos instead of this
collection of yelling thoughts now gnawing his attention.
Anyone can only handle so much; once that limit is
reached, only madness remains. Fingertips frayed and sent
shockwaves of pain every few seconds, knees now starting
to bleed from the constant friction while only being able to
crawl in this tight space, which seemed to be getting
progressively smaller with the entry of each new room. The
list of discomforts outweighed his functionality, and one
more had been added to the list—a full bladder that felt as
if it was ready to burst at any moment.

A massive piss was probably the only relief he was going
to get for a while, so Elias picked a corner a few rooms
behind the current one he now took residence in and let go
of a giant splashing stream of urine which was pungent and
starting to pool towards the makeshift weld job that
conjoined both containers. "FUCK, what did I drink?"

An aroma redolent of pennies and old pickle juice
permeated the air, giving off the type of miasma that could
turn even the strongest stomach.

"That stinks so bad!" Elias could not escape the smell he
was now trapped with, like an unbathed passenger on a bus
with their stench-laden seat right next to his for a lengthy
ride. He looked up at the new wall and noticed it had

writing in that familiar red ink: "HOPE YOU'RE HUNGRY!" This was the absolute last thing on his mind, especially given that now a puddle of warm piss was brewing in the dusty heat nearby; the urge to break this wall was somehow more tremendous to evade that heavy fragrance wafting of its own accord throughout this tight quartered shell.

With a consistent flaring of his nostrils and strong stomach from years of working on rooves, breathing in the tar mixture that hung in the summer air of many long days, he was able to handle just about anything that meandered in and out of his lungs and sinuses without being too heavily affected. Finally— roofing had its benefits after all. Elias went to carve into the next wall while gripping his knife with bandaged hands that started to resemble the tattered wrappings of a mummified corpse buried in some sarcophagus. It was not hard to feel like he identified with those poor bastards at this point in time. "Another double wall," he said with an extreme sense of exhaustion from a severe lack of energy, most likely—although he was never going to admit it— from hunger.

As he knocked down a large piece of wall, a sucker punch of rot hit his nasal cavity and breached his resolve while simultaneously rekindling his long dormant gag reflex, iron stomach be damned. The wretch hung in his throat with a solid ferocity, a lump of bile waiting to be unleashed from its esophageal confines. What he saw on the other side of the wall were several takeout containers filled and hanging by strings above the makeshift tunnel floors; a few remnants of what looked like Chinese takeout had spilled from several of the suspended boxes. This was a fetor that far surpassed his puddle of waste; a stinging of sinuses mixed with a swarm of flies greeted him in this wonderful new room that happened to be the only way to get to the other end of this maze.

The threads holding the damp and musty cardboard containers above were starting to fray as they were bombarded with common house flies and an assortment of maggots who basked in the globs of decay which hung and swayed by fragile swinging strands, pushing them to their absolute brink— Elias could relate.

He tried a new method of breathing, which involved small open-mouthed gasps to avoid taking in any of the unpleasant scent of the rotting garbage ahead. A mouth swelling full of spittle as salivatory glands exhausted themselves reacting to the pungent aroma of refuse savagely assaulting his senses. This sour filth never ceased and made itself known, an invasive essence whose omnipresence devoured all it surrounded.
Miasma of what could only be identified as weeks-old Chinese food was only the beginning of his most recent dilemma; the flies that now were swarming the tunnel became another unwanted obstacle to contend with on his way through this medley of plights strewn together to choke him out and level his resolve constantly.

As the rest of the wall was cut, Elias covered his nose with the antecubital fossa of the arm that he currently held the flashlight in; there was always a focused positioning of the beam of light that was now dim and orange in hue, a piece of the moon he carried with him to make his eternal darkness just a minuscule amount more endurable, the literal beacon of hope he grasped tightly like the hand of a loved one.

This made him reminisce about the times he would walk in a park as a child while holding tightly onto his mother's hand; in those moments, he was invincible; nothing horrific or terrifying could get him once he held his mother's tender palm. A feeling that there had never been an equal to, until this moment with this item, which was temporarily illuminating a path for him. Almost as if his mother was carving a way through the blackness for him to see that he could make it out of this in one piece. After a while, Elias started to believe this to be true — there was no way all of this would crush him.

The flies kept swarming, and the putrid garbage now permeated through all means to try and block its obstructive punch. None of this could shake Elias out of his thoughts to deduce what he needed to do next while also reflecting on times past. He wanted to solve what led him down a painful road that had him scratching and clawing for substances for many years of his life.
After the prolonged period of cerebral travel— a depth of thinking that Elias did as a means of involuntary disassociation— a cathartic embrace that had been his constant companion in a world that he felt would shun him, never gaining the courage to speak to anyone about his

internal struggles. There were flashes at times that smothered his present thoughts, thoughts of a father who was an abusive alcoholic who used him as a punching bag whenever his work days became too arduous.

More of the wall was cut away, some disintegrating while clumping into a substance resembling a chalky porridge. On impact with the ground, the billowing smog of harsh toxins rushes by, scattering the swarming flies, and the air becomes once again thick with a powder-like taste. This had been less of a lung-ruining duvet covering Elias while also blinding; this was more manageable somehow; the wall crumbled a bit differently, holding the shape but still shattering like the others. This partition was damp. The festering trash had created a mold-ridden, humid biome where insects flourished. A hanging garden of cantankerous boxes filled with brown noodle-like masses and crawling with maggots. It was sticky and warm, like the inside of a sewage drain; in fact, the smell gave off a similar resemblance.

This warm compost heap generated so much natural heat from decomposition that it started to make Elias sweat. The wall around the brown recycled hanging takeout containers was moist with condensation. As he had suspected, things in this awful tunnel had taken a severe turn for the worse. Clumps of scattered detritus littered the once wooden floor, turning it into a rubble pile similar to a small landfill; the swarm of flies that seemed to become blinded by the mostly dark scenery smacked into Elias' face repeatedly. Swinging above his head now are the almost steaming boxes of rotting food, which overflowed with dropping maggots, some of which were now falling on his head and squirming through his hair. This entire room made that lump in his throat give way, making him launch a large amount of projectile vomit all over one of the walls." Pity, this place was gorgeous before I spilled my guts," a thought that entered his mind as a possible defense mechanism deflecting his rational mind from fully comprehending the absolute vile hole he was now crawling through.

The hermetic seal in the steel frame made the rancidity of the waste around him inescapable. The modified breathing pattern he had applied started to cause a slight bit of light-headedness, and his mouth constantly watered as more upheaval seemed inevitable while wading through pounds of the maggot-ridden scrap heap, watching as his hands plunged into more of the brown offal. Elias felt the acrid mud-like scum scoop under the fingernails still exposed despite being wrapped in now stained and soiled strips which loosely held on hands. The flies became the most considerable nuisance in this awful compression chamber; they flew into every orifice or area that was open or available, Elias was starting to feel like they wanted to crawl in his mouth to escape the smell themselves, but these horrible bastards eat and surround shit— so they had no excuse.

The sludge from the rotten food had accumulated on his hands and knees to the point that he started to lose solid traction; the congealed fats and gelatinous mass of greenish gravy-like textures made Elias begin to slide a bit, teasing a very unwanted faceplant right into the dregs if his balance were to not be corrected soon. The involuntary sliding started to propel him forward slightly through the room while also not making him as stable as he would have been in a less soggy bog of spoiled food. With a decent center of gravity and a modicum of inertia, Elias was able to keep both his balance and his face away from the depths of this leftover-filled enclosure.

Bracing for an inevitable submergence in the filth that pooled below him while bathing in the cantankerous food boxes that hung above him, Elias was in a precarious waste sandwich while crawling toward the next wall. His stomach, however, could no longer hold back the accumulation of vomit he had amassed in his esophagus, and like a levy that had seen one too many hurricanes, he projected a river of bile and whatever contents he had left swimming in his stomach in one giant lumpy puddle. This new liquid mass coalesced with the already insufferable amount of viscous slime beneath his hands and feet as he clawed his way further into the incomprehensible mess.

His head moved upward involuntarily, triggering another suspended food container to unleash its spoiled sludge all over his head. As he felt it slide down his face, the rotten muck was crawling, with more maggots taking a ride on what used to be udon noodles right into Elias' open mouth.

A spasming gyration and continuous spitting followed as the creeping pests could be felt crawling all over his chest and legs. He was now flailing to get rid of his unwanted residents who were trying to catch a ride with him to the next room. Through these violent motions, followed by repulsed screams, he caused another suspended container to fall and splash decaying juices all over him once again; this made him stay in a state of stasis to assess the room more competently. He had to keep progressing, though, despite becoming the equivalent of puss in an infected wound.

Maggots continued to wriggle through the apertures between his fingers as the flies swarmed once again, sometimes landing on his tongue still covered in the remnants of what he was sifting through to inch his way to the opposite end of this endeavor. Open-mouth breathing was now proving to be much more difficult because of the sheer number of flies trying to find any other home outside this nightmare.

And then it happened...

Darkness.

The flashlight cut out, and all Elias was left with was the slimy sensations of insects surrounding him as he swam through sticky garbage to make a clearing for a wall that seemed to be miles away.

Tom Harmon

Lisa Tomey-Zonneveld is the founder/manager of Prolific Pulse Press LLC and a widely published poet and writer. She is an editor of numerous anthologies and for Fine Lines Journal. She is Poet Laureate Emeritus of Garden of Neuro Institute and is an organizer for Living Poetry in North Carolina. ProlificPulse.blog

Cardinal Dreams

Gathering up his son's clothes, scattered about the bedroom floor, Daniel watched over his slumbering son. Jeffrey lay with his ball glove secured in hand. His signed baseball had rolled off onto the blanket. Hair tousled in rings of curls, he slumbered away with little boy dreams.

Not long before, Daniel and Jeffrey were spectators at their very first Saint Louis Cardinals baseball game. This was a dream realized when Jeffrey's grandparents surprised him with tickets on his birthday. Daniel was even more excited than Jeffrey and immediately made plans for the big event.

As Albert Pujols stood, ready to give it his all, the fans chanted "Batter, batter," expecting him to hit a homer each time. Having watched Pujols play religiously, Daniel was ready to enlist his sidekick, Jeffrey, as part of the fan base.

Daniel laid all of Jeffrey's clothes out for the next day. Before leaving his room and preparing for his own day to come, he packed lunches, paid bills, and made certain there was nothing left undone before a new day.

Falling into a deep sleep, Daniel drifted into a dream state. He fell deeper than he had known in a long time, perhaps since she was by his side, before, well, before she drifted off and didn't wake up. Daniel dreamed he was at Busch Stadium. Tiffany was by his side and Jeffrey was on her lap. Watching the pre-game activities, he gazed into her eyes and winked at her as she bounced Jeffrey on her knee. Tiffany smiled back, and then looked at their son as he babbled in baby talk, obviously having a gleeful time.

Waking from his sleep, Daniel wiped the tears from his eyes, then got up to check on Jeffrey, who was still soundly sleeping. Placing his hand on his son's head, he said a prayer. Thinking of Tiffany's smile, he went back to bed, hopeful of finding her by his side again.

Love Knots

Her matron of honor worked the bride's hair into love knots,
adorned with ribbons of blue.
Her mother gently rubbed knots from her daughter's hair
to allow her nightly brush.
She tied her shoes in double knots so she could run
without tripped strings and skinned knees.
She felt knots in her stomach when she experienced her
first kiss,
from the equally knotted boy.
Clover was joined in love knots, to create a crown
for her pretend wedding at aged six.
All decked out for her first infant show, she cooed
as her mother adorned her hair with ribbons of blue.

Band on the Run, Again
How about a redo, friend
when the band can run and play again.
A reunion it would be, fresh as 1973.
Spinning vinyl playing anthems
saluting the fact that they have returned.
Oh to go back in time,
rewind
to band on the run, again.

Freedom Flight
Formed in the image of a butterfly
she was winged with spirit, to propel.
Her heart took to flight.
It soared in unison to the flow of the breeze,
tickling flowers,
delight in being free.
She found the essence of life.

 space above my head
dragonfly hovers over my head
keeps a distance of closeness in space
my wonder is what he might be thinking
perhaps a desire to buss my cheek
or weave a nest from my whispy hair
he in his place and I in mine, we keep perfect time

Lisa Tomey-Zonneveld

125

Don Vaughan is a freelance writer based in Raleigh, North Carolina, and the founder of Triangle Association of Freelancers.

World's Greatest Burger

The girl exited the taxi a half block from the bustling restaurant and walked the rest of the way. The place was packed with ravers and other late-night denizens desperate for something grilled and greasy. No one recognized her. At the sidewalk counter she ordered a burger combo, heavy onions, tots fried hard, and a chocolate shake, triple scoop.

She stood to one side as her order was prepared, scrolling through her phone. A floppy hat and lightly tinted glasses carefully hid her features. To anyone passing by, she was just another pretty blonde among many.

When her name was called, the girl picked up her tray and walked into the seating area. It, too, was packed, and she swore under her breath. She was about to head outside in search of an empty bench when she spotted the lone vacant chair, a chrome-and-plastic siren that seemed to call only to her. She ran to it, placed her tray heavily on the small table and dropped into the chair with a grunt.

"Hi, there!" said the man she hadn't noticed.

"Oh shit!" The girl scooted backward in cartoon-character fashion, nearly knocking her tray to the floor. "I am so sorry! I didn't see you! I'll go outside…"

"No, no, please stay," the man said, gesturing to the empty chair. "Really, it's fine. I'd love the company." His smile put the girl at ease.

"Thank you so much, it's nuts here tonight." The girl slid back into her chair and unwrapped her hamburger.

"I'm Ed, by the way."

"Nice to meet you. I'm Jenny."

They dug in. After a few moments, Ed said, "You…look kinda familiar. I swear I know you from somewhere."

Jenny gave a weak shrug.

Suddenly, Ed's eyes grew wide in recognition. "Oh my God!"

Jenny looked at him plaintively, eyes wide. "Please, I just want to enjoy a hamburger without it being a thing," she whispered. "Please don't draw attention!"

"You're Tammi Silver."

Jenny hesitated. "Yes."

"I'm sorry. I didn't mean to react that way. It's just…"

"It's okay. Luckily, no one's paying attention."

"My daughter, Kate, has your CD. She listens to it constantly."

"Which one?"

"I… I don't know," Ed said awkwardly. "I know who you are, I mean, I've seen you on TV and everything. But I'm embarrassed to say that I don't really know much about your music. I'm more of a classic rock guy."
Jenny laughed. "That's okay. The parents of most of my fans couldn't name one of my albums either. How old is your daughter?"

"Eleven. We also have a three-year-old son, Caleb. Jenn… do you prefer to be called Jenny or Tammi?"
"My friends call me Jenny. Jennifer is my actual first name."
"If you don't mind me asking, Jenny, why are you here?"
"I needed a World's Greatest Burger."
"I mean New York."

"Oh. I'm performing three shows at the Garden this weekend. The first one was tonight. And what about you? What brings you to World's Greatest Burger at two in the morning?" Without comment she reached over and casually wiped a dollop of catsup off of Ed's cheek.

"After-work snack. I'm a unit nurse at a skilled nursing facility a few blocks from here on 87th, and one of my staff had a family emergency so I took their shift. I thought it would be better to eat here than wake my wife fixing something when I get home. How about you? Wouldn't it have been easier just to have one of your people come here and bring a burger back for you?"

"And eat it cold? No. A World's Greatest Burger must be eaten fresh off the grill, you know that. So, I got dressed, snuck past my security people, paid the desk clerk a hundred bucks to call me a cab, with the promise of a selfie and another hundred if she promised not to call the press, and here I am."

"So, you paid two hundred and twenty-five dollars for a hamburger."
"A hamburger with tots and a shake," Jenny corrected. "And it's worth every penny."
"You lead a very unusual life," Ed observed with a smile. "What's it like…"

"Being Tammi Silver?" It was a question Jenny had obviously heard many times before. "It's hectic and stressful and exhausting and tremendous fun and really exciting. Tonight, I performed before nineteen thousand screaming fans. Not a lot of people ever get that experience."

"This sounds weird, I know, but you seem pretty…normal." Jenny laughed.
"I'm really lucky. My parents have always supported my singing, and they head my management team. They make sure I keep my shit together, and shelter me from some of the nastier aspects of the industry. That's why I'm normal."

"How old are you?"

"Twenty-six. You?

"Forty-two."

They ate in silence for a moment, then Jenny said, "Tell me more about your job. Isn't it depressing working in a nursing home?"

"Skilled nursing facility," Ed said. "And yes, it can be a little depressing sometimes. You become very attached to the residents, and when they pass, it's almost like losing a member of the family. They have so many stories to tell, if you're willing to listen. I found out last week that one of the men on my floor was part of the initial landing force at Normandy during D-Day. I've known him for three years, and I had no idea until he just dropped that little nugget while I was helping him with his shower."

"How do you handle it when one of the patients dies? That must be really hard."

"When someone dies, we hold a facility-wide commemorative service for them. We talk about them, share photos. That's one of the things that makes St. Mark's unique. And one of the reasons I really like my job."

"Does your wife work there too?"

"No, Miranda's an elementary school teacher. She's taught third grade for fourteen years."

"I wanted to be a teacher when I was younger," Jenny said wistfully. "I love kids."

"They can be a handful," Ed said. "Thankfully, Miranda's mother is available to help out." He paused for a tot.

"Jenny, how the heck do you handle your fame? It's like you're never alone, and it all sounds terrifying to me."

"Fame – my level of fame -- has its perks, but it also comes with a lot of restrictions that most people don't think about," Jenny said. "That's something the head of my security team told me at the start of my very first tour, and he was right. I make a lot of money, true. But I can't go shopping in public or to the movies with friends. When I go out to a restaurant, I have to eat in a back room with security at the door. I'm very happy with my life, but it can be difficult."

She glanced at her burger, then directly into Ed's eyes for the first time. "The worst part is my fans. I love them, and I know they love me, but I am in constant danger because of them. If the crowd in this restaurant right now became aware of who you're with, we would immediately be swarmed and probably get hurt. Not on purpose, but the mob mentality at a celebrity sighting can be a frightening thing. I've seen it happen a couple of times, when some aspect of my security failed and the crowds got too close. I was genuinely afraid, Ed. And those were the fans who like me. My security team screens my mail and reports the most dangerous threats to the FBI."

Ed was stunned. "You get a lot of those?"

"Several a week. I try not to think about it, and let my security people do their job." The expression on her face told Ed that Jenny was telling him things she had never told anyone outside of her immediate circle. He felt like her therapist.

"When did you start singing?" Ed felt the need to change the subject.
"When I was eleven. I started singing in church."
"What was your first experience singing in public?"
"A talent show at the mall in my home town when I was fourteen. I came in twelfth."
"That's not so bad."
"There were fourteen contestants." Jenny laughed loudly at the memory. "Things got better."

Ed and Jenny finished their meals at almost the same time. Hungry people carrying burger-laden trays prowled the seating area like wolves.

"I should be getting back," Jenny said. "Ed, please don't tell anyone that you met me here tonight. It would be a huge headache for me if that got out, and there's a good chance the paparazzi would be all over you and your family, which you do not want, believe me."

"Not a word," Ed promised. "Can I walk you out? I'll stay with you until you get a taxi."

The crowd outside had grown larger and the scent of grilled meat and fried tots filled the air. "Would you put your arm around me?" Jenny asked. "That makes us more invisible." Ed complied, gently putting his arm around Jenny's waist as if they were a couple. A few moments later, a taxi swerved to the curb. Jenny got in and gave the driver the name of her hotel. "Thank you for a wonderful dinner, Ed! It was a pleasure meeting you."

"Back atcha," Ed said with a smile. "We'll have to do it again sometime." With that, the most famous singer in the world disappeared into late-night traffic. Ed walked to the subway station and found himself home twenty minutes later. He undressed and climbed into bed, taking care to not wake Miranda, who was snoring gently beneath the covers. The black service car pulled up in front of their brownstone around 11 a.m. the next morning, as Ed and Miranda prepared to go grocery shopping. Miranda answered the door. "Are you Miranda Dougherty?" the driver asked. Miranda nodded, and the man handed her a beautifully wrapped box. With a smile, he returned to the car and drove away.

Inside the box were four front-row tickets to that evening's Tammi Silver concert at the Garden.
Miranda looked at Ed. "I had dinner last night with Tammi Silver," he confessed. "I stopped at World's Greatest Burger before coming home, and she accidentally sat down at my table because she thought it was empty. She was all by herself, and had snuck out of her hotel because she was hungry. I guess the tickets are her way of saying thanks for

not being an asshole and just treating her like a normal person. She must have called St. Mark's for our address."

"Are you serious? Why didn't you tell me?!"

"She asked me not to. She was concerned that if news of our dinner together got out, it could cause problems for her and for us, so I thought it was just better not to say anything. I guess she changed her mind."
Ed picked up the tickets, and beneath them saw a small envelope with a card inside. It read simply, "Hope you and your family can make it. PS: I got busted by my security! Jenny." There was a smiley face.

"What are we going to do?" Miranda asked.

"I guess we're going to see Tammi silver at the Garden tonight. Wait until Kate finds out, she's gonna freak! Let's call your mom and see if she can watch Caleb."
Kate was speechless when casually presented with the concert tickets, then she burst into tears. When she invited her best friend, Andrea, to join them, the girls' screams could be heard across the street.

The tickets really were for the front row. But as they settled in, a man in a black jacket approached Ed. "I'm truly sorry, sir, but there's been a mistake regarding your seats."

"I don't understand," Ed said. "These are the seat numbers on our tickets."

"Tammi has asked that you enjoy the show from the stage," the man said.

"Excuse me?"

"Your seats are up there," the man said, pointing. "Please come with me."

Kate and Andrea simply stared at each other as they were escorted behind the massive set and into an area from which they could see the entire show unobstructed. A few others were already seated there. A man in white gloves approached and asked if they wanted a beverage. Ed looked at his family. Miranda shrugged. "Four Cokes, please," Ed said.

Shortly before the show, Tammi joined the backstage group, which was comprised mostly of industry bigwigs and their families. She was dressed in a gold jumpsuit and was wearing heavy makeup. She chatted with the others first, then came over to Ed and his family. "You must be Kate!" she said, giving the stunned 11-year-old a tight hug.

"Your dad told me you're a big fan, so I really hope you enjoy the show. Would you like a selfie?" Kate immediately produced her cell phone and she, Andrea and Tammi squeezed together for a picture. "I'll also make sure you receive an autographed photo after the show," Jenny said. "I need to get ready, so I have to go."
Ten minutes later, lasers split the darkness and Tammi Silver took the stage to the opening strains of her most

recent hit. The mostly prepubescent crowd screamed so loudly that even back stage, Ed sometimes had difficulty hearing her sing. The concert lasted two hours and fifteen minutes, during which Tammi sang a total of 18 songs over five costume changes.

As Tammi performed the final song of the night, the man who had escorted them backstage appeared with an envelope. Inside were autographed photos for Kate and Andrea, and a note for Miranda, reading, "You're married to a wonderful man. I hope I'm as lucky someday." Miranda reached over and softly squeezed her husband's hand. To her left, Kate held Tammi's photo tightly to her chest as she sang as loudly as she could.

Don Vaughan

K Ann Pennington is fascinated by the constructed nature of place in America. She focuses specifically on primary source materials and performing field research on a variety of topics, especially the Civil War. More about K Ann's stories can be found at:
https://kannpennington.wordpress.com/

He'd Survived Vietnam

"C'mon, Bradbury. Sly, we're going!" I slammed the door.

Marlene could get bent. How FUBAR was it of her to leave me when she knew what had happened? What a contemptible rag she was? I threw my bag in the trunk, dropped the cold sixer in the icy cooler, and let Sly leap into the passenger seat.

"Another adventure, buddy. This time, we're gonna be where we belong. Where we shoulda been."
Sly licked my face in agreement. Bradbury loved Sly, but it hadn't been enough to keep Bradbury from leaving, too.
I threw the stick in reverse and backed up my Datsun 240Z, not in an angry way, but a determined one, and I sped off the same.

"Our" place in the rearview.
"It was such a joke, Sly!"

Yea, bye. Flatland didn't do much for me anyway. The place literally stunk. By the time I got to Miamuh, OK, the stupid little wooden bungalows in a row irritated me. I

137

stopped in a vacant weedy lot by one of them and let Sly out to piss on its bushes. We walked a little; he got burrstickers in his pads and I had to pick them out. Muttered "place is a crapdump" but knew I got what I deserved.

"My fault, Sly, I'm sorry," I said as I loaded my buddy into the car and gave him another pet.
I survived the Oklahoma City Crosstown Expressway and crossed the old Chisholm Trail, thinking about Bradbury acting out westerns and me emulating him with Dad's cowboy boots on. I hadn't been given a pair yet, but Bradbury had. And he'd loved his guns then as he did when he got older. I knew it would be a gun.
Western Oklahoma and more flat land. Lots of gospel and cattle prices on the AM.
Bored; barely keeping eyes open, until I saw a neon sign that appealed to me more than the rest. "Lamplighter Motel," it said in soft orange and green, alluring me with coziness Sly gave it his stamp of approval by squeaking two times with his mouth shut, and I swerved into the lot and rented a room. Out of the car and on the loose with no leash, he urinated on three different bushes within close proximity to one another without me asking him to, then he led me to the strip of doors despite not knowing which one was ours.
In the room, I dropped my bag on the sagging bed. I worried Sly still had stickers on him and inspected his body during the gentle bath I gave him before I showered.
"We're getting up before dawn, so don't be a putz when the time comes. You can sleep it off in the car."

138

Knowing he'd been given instructions, Sly stared into my
eyes, then put his head down, but never averted his gaze
from me.

"I love you, buddy. So much."
He still looked at me. I fed him, then I ate my sandwich
and drank my beer. I burped after the final chug. Sly
sniffed the air I made. I let him out for last piss.

***

I had a breakfast of three little beef-stuffed corn tacos and a
cup of black coffee to keep my tired eyes open. Last night,
Sly had taken up most of the little bed; the mattress
slumped in the middle, and Sly stretched out in its lowest
point. And the Magic Fingers turned on by itself, so we
vibrated with me close to the edge of the bed for about an
hour, then it shut off. I guess I slept after that.

Drove along crops and more crops in west
Oklahoma. On the radio, students at Kent State had been
shot. Early reports said some were killed. National Guard
and guns.

I thought about Bradbury never having to feel hated
again, and I hoped he hadn't taken that feeling with him
when he left.

"Sly, when we get there, no women, okay? Don't
let me. Don't attract anyone at the beach or downtown.
You must be my anti-battery radar."

Sly's pant broke with a grin in my direction, then he
stared straight ahead.

"Hard not to be irresistible, huh, buddy?"
Tucumcari, New Mexico had a motel, "The Cactus," that
seemed fine. In room number three, I felt it getting closer;

139

I cried. Sly sat by me. Outside, the neon sign buzzed, pulsating with the rhythm of alternating desert red and cactus green. Bradbury always hated that kind of sound. He said it put him back under the Hueys that approached the LZs.

I showered and tried to rinse off my cares, but I couldn't. If only I hadn't—

"I'm toweling off! I don't miss Marlene!" I yelled out facts to keep from losing it. And regulated the breathing through my nose and mouth.

But, just Bradbury. I only missed him. Oh, god—Sly barked.

I peered through my tears; he stared at my bag and barked again. I checked around the room and outside the door. No one was there. Sly curled up into a ball on the bed, a sign he wanted to be covered and allowed to sleep. He'd barked for me, and I took the cue and pulled myself together. Bradbury didn't want me as a puddling mess, either.

***

I stopped at the Tucumcari pharmacy to get a Coke for breakfast on my way out of town.
By Williams, empty flatlands of my past had been replaced by rocky edges of the Continental Divide. Protests covered by the press made sharp sounds to accompany the landscape. I felt distant from the chaos, whereas, in Chicago, we'd been near it.

Kent students and Bradbury and guns.
Somehow, being unattached and in the middle of nowhere Arizona brought me piece of mind; I didn't want to live there, but I let the place wash over me as I passed through

it. My quiet and the mountains made me tiny and my problems small, especially in light of Kent State, although I'd seen someone dead on the ground, too. And they, too, had been young.

I ate Mexican food at Cline's Corners, a turquoise travel stand dominating the four-way intersection of roads—lonely roads that went on for miles until they met the mountains.

Sly loved peeing in the desert. We'd pull over, take a walk, and he'd find relief, and even get hollered at from under a yucca by a rattler's maraca.

The Sierra came on the horizon like a giant loving mother, welcoming us with her bosomy embrace. I'd driven for miles to reach her, but she'd kept inching away—until she was upon us!

And then I got up to Route 58 and cranked Zeppelin. The road lifted me with the music, up past McKittrick, up into the hills clinging to their green but also turning to straw, up through the canyons and far above the creek carving California gold. Bradbury wanted so desperately to feel California gold again.

Sly licked the sweet air; he'd never smelled The Golden State, and certainly not an ocean.

"We're home, buddy. I'm finally home."

We emerged from the western-facing side of the coastal range at Santa Margarita, and I lead-footed it to San Luis Obispo. I knew where the fuzz would be, when to slow, and when it was safe to open 'er up.

"You're about to visit the most magical place in the world, Sly." I felt my eyes get wet. "For frack's sake, why do I cry so much lately?"

I'd begun to use "frack" around Mom, too. Bradbury used to say it because Mom didn't like us cussing. But right before Bradbury and I went to the Big Nam, we cut loose. We'd cuss in front of Mom to make her yell at us, then we'd laugh.

Mom told me a few months ago she'd give anything to hear him cuss again, she'd even join in the laughter. So I cussed for her now and then.

Sly leaned toward me; he always did when I got wrapped up in it like that.

"I'd love to pet you, buddy. Thank you."
San Luis Obispo appeared the same as I remembered, especially Fire station Number One and bustling Main Street.

"Where Bradbury and I were born and raised."
Sly sat up taller, repositioning his front feet as if he understood the importance.

"Are you ready for the beach? And I don't mean a great lake beach. I mean the ocean."

His eyes darted around, checking the water, me, other people, the water again; his ears twitched. He stood up on the armrest and stuck his head out the window, looking right at people we passed. Some said "Hi" to him and "Aw, how cute?"

In Morro Bay, we parked by the sea and I walked Sly to Morro Rock.

"I surfed here, buddy. Spent all my free time here. With Bradbury."

I took Sly to a private spot only local surfers knew. There, I let him off the leash; no sets rolled in, but the water swished to speak its gentle word.

Sly splashed around, unaware that I'd taken the baggie from the small box that I'd carried in my bag. I opened the baggie and said toward it, "Welcome home, brother. I'm sorry I took a year to get you here. Suppose I had to get my head straight about it, but no way I'd have left you in Chicago. I see it now: I'd waited for this chance to do it right. I know you love this place."

I let the contents of the baggie fly on the sweet breeze. A light gust sprayed some of Bradbury all over me and Sly, and the water. The air stilled, and Bradbury settled on the current. He became taken in and taken in, until I saw more water and less Bradbury, until none of Bradbury remained. Now that he'd been made one with Morro Bay, Bradbury would at once touch everywhere and be home.

Sly bounced to me, disrupting little blue eddies.

"Thank you, buddy." I crouched close to him and stroked his wet head fur. Water splashed me in playful ways. Sly licked my salty face.

"You need water. I've got to find us a job and somewhere to live." I stared at ripples flirting with the shore; unlike them, I felt unable to pull away and end that moment there with Bradbury. Our spirits had met in the surf of our old beach. We shared the gold.

I breathed in the air of him and home and my salty dog, and finally smiled.

The Count

Once more reaching over
For my four-leaf clover
Hoping you'll return again someday

I miss you; moreover,
forever waiting on my clover,
I've eyes for no one else but you

You're my lucky seven,
though miles away in heaven,
watching down to make sure I'm okay

Oh, my charmed three,
Behind all that I see
light the dark and turn skies blue from gray

But endless hills of clover,
on none do I discover,
leaves of four that lead you home to me

For our world's Great Composer
choses those who bide lower
and those risen to the reflection of the sea.

K Ann Pennington

Arlene S. Bice is a writer of local history (NJ), poetry, metaphysics, memoir, fiction, and short stories. This story is from her most recent book, Rumors and Other Short Stories. Her website is: arlenebice.com   She lives in Farmville, Virginia.

The Ivory Silk Peignoir Set
*In memory of Anne Dippold Peterson

Anne works as a companion to an elderly woman in a senior living community for folks who have lots of money to smooth the cares of their last years on earth. It's demanding on her, especially mentally, but she's naturally good at it because she has a nurturing demeanor. She cares. And it shows.

It shows so obviously that one day on Anne's entrance across the wide verandah of the Italianate house into the elegant receiving room, one of the women rose from her Victorian chair and reached out to tug on her sleeve.

"Anne, please come into my apartment for a moment before going to Charlotte's. I want to ask you something."

"Of course," she replied as she slowly followed down the thickly carpeted hallway to Miss Sydney's apartment.

As soon as Anne stepped into the room Miss Sydney picked up a dress box sitting on the entrance table and placed it into her hands. Saks Fifth Avenue, New York was printed in faded gold lettering on the lid. The corners were nicked like it had been carried from place to place before being stored away but not forgotten. A bit of white tissue paper stuck out of the side. She didn't open it since Miss Sydney had not released it. She just held it there like it was an envelope at the Oscar Awards in Hollywood. Secret. Treasured. Sought after.

"Would you stop in before you leave for home today? I'll make us a nice pot of tea. I want to tell you about this and why I want you to have it." She still didn't open it or let it out of her hands, just waited for Anne to answer."

Unable to deny her favorite resident of the Maplewood Gardens Anne agreed delightfully.

Out of twelve women Anne came in contact with daily, Miss Sydney was a favorite. Three men joined in the same group. While Anne was hired to tend to just one, they all gathered, a few with companions, most not, for meals, planned activities, and light entertainment. As in any group many personalities emerged. Miss Sydney's refined background stood out as boldly as she was gracious. It's the breeding. Shows every time.

The scent of JOY touched the room. Anne thought of Miss Sydney telling her the story of her favorite perfume. She never mentioned the price tag on it though. Being a collector of fine antique perfume bottles and out of curiosity, Anne researched it. One could always tell "old money."

Frenchman Jean Patou created JOY in 1930 specifically for his many wealthy American couture customers. When the stock market crashed in 1929 he lost most of those customers in his designer line, but they returned to buy the perfume toted as nearly the most expensive perfume in the world. He produced only one more scent, the expensive "1000." Not liked by Miss Sydney. She preferred JOY with its flowery, feminine scent made from the blending of natural, precious rose and jasmine oils. Jean Patou passed away in 1936.

Even though the perfume was recommended for evening wear Miss Sydney touched it lightly to her wrists each morning. The Eau De Parfum Spray sold for $90 an ounce. Anne agreed and left to attend her charge.

As promised, when Anne finished with Charlotte, she tapped on Miss Sydney's door. Entering, her eyes went right to the dressed round table in the alcove set with tea things. The damask tablecloth fell in soft folds to the floor. On top of the table were an Artois Bleu Bernardaud Tea Pot with matching cups, dessert plates, and accessories.

Careful not to let her mouth drop open, Anne recognized the exquisite French porcelain with the delicate floral design. Her grandmother came from France and brought the same fine china tea pot with her. But not the matching pieces. Anne knew she was sitting down to a thousand dollar "Tea" before she even checked over the delicacies.

As Anne's eyes absorbed the beautiful pastries and tea sandwiches her mind wandered to Limoges, the area in France where this wonderful porcelain came from.

"Miss Sydney." Anne addressed her even though her name was really Mrs. Randolph. She liked the old southern custom of using her given name with the old title of respect, Miss.

"Let me tell you of my familiarity with your Bernardaud china. A Baron with the first name of Anne started the porcelain business there in the 1700s. In the next century my grandmother was an artist, painting on Limoges china. I have a few pieces of hers that I cherish dearly. I've even wondered if I were named for that Baron." Anne beamed with a quiet pride.

"I'm delighted that you recognize it. There are many wealthy people here but only a few are aware of my treasures, as I call them. Please sit down and be comfortable. There's no need to rush home tonight, is there?"

"No, I'm yours for as long as you like. There's no hot date waiting for me." They both chuckled.

Miss Sydney made small talk while she poured the tea and passed the tray. Her mind was working as if to put her thoughts in place before speaking. Settling down with the taste of cucumber and cream cheese fresh in her mouth, Miss Sydney began.

"I've told you bits and pieces about my Randolph and how we met in 1945 during the War. He was a Captain then."

A smile spread over her face as it always did when she spoke of the born-and-raised-Virginian. Pictures of him were lavishly spread around the charming room. One was of him sitting his horse in Middleburg, Virginia next to a young, lovely Jackie Kennedy astraddle on her own horse.

"I was an army nurse at that time. I loved him so." She continued. "Good far outweighed any downs in our life together. I realize how fortunate I've been. I've written our story including the photos we've taken over all these years for the children and grandchildren, etc. I think they should know us as we were. Not just as parents and grandparents."

She paused as she sipped her tea and refreshed mine.

"There's an earlier story that I want to tell but it's not for my family. I've been waiting for the right person who'll listen without bias that will appreciate it, keep it so it won't die. That's important to me."

Again, Miss Sydney paused, sure of what she was doing but still hesitant to let go. That's the hard part. Letting go.

Anne sat quietly with her usual patience and tenderness circling her air. She knew the time was for her to listen, not talk, not even comment. A nod of the head was sufficient to let Miss Sydney know she was with her.

"I've come to know you in this last year as I've watched you without your realizing it. I'm very impressed with your sensitivity towards the old folks here. If I needed a personal assistant I would ask you and certainly hope you would agree. But I don't."

With that said she rose, pulled open a drawer from the sideboard bringing out the dress box from earlier in the day. She sat down, opened it, folded back the white tissue paper so gently as if it might disintegrate in her tiny fingers. It was obviously old, yet the paper still crinkled when she handled it.

"What's this Miss Sydney?" Anne smiled while slowly rising. She approached her as she raised a lovely ivory silk peignoir set, with vintage lace worked in. Silence

149

lay on the room like a featherbed on fresh sheets. The soft ticking of the porcelain clock on the mantel revealed the only sign of life. No other sound entered the room while Anne quietly sat down again and waited for the tiny, delicate crone to rouse herself from wherever she had gone mentally.

A deep breath, a sigh, and Miss Sydney whispered "it's time. Here is my story."

"Beau Davis and I first met when he moved into my small town in Georgia where I was born and raised. It was love at first sight. I was a 12 year old southern belle to his city boy of 14. He was a breath of fresh air, dashing, smart, and sophisticated, to me anyway. We spent as much time as possible together all through our teen years until the Japanese bombed Pearl Harbor one Sunday morning. It was exactly one week before our proposed wedding day. Beau Davis enlisted Monday morning, December 8. Never said a word to me, just did it, telling me we would get married when he returned.

"He was good at writing letters, reminding me of our love and speaking of future plans when he came home. They stopped arriving in March of 1942. Shortly after the telegram came that he was missing in action.

"I grieved. Oh, I grieved thinking my life had ended when Beau Davis was gone. I never expected to lose him in the war. I really didn't.

As soon as he left for boot camp, I took schooling in nursing. It wasn't something I planned to do when I thought I was going to major in wife and mother duties. I volunteered for European duty hoping to learn something about my Beau Davis. A bit of a silly thought, that one; I had no clue how big the world really was.

"As time wore on the devastation of our troops filled up the hole within me. I worked until I couldn't stand up, slept, and went back to the field again. Wherever they sent me was okay. I made a couple of lifelong nurse friends that I loved like sisters I didn't have at home. With all the killing it was important to find someone to love and then pray they weren't killed. We often were close to the actual fighting.

"Letters from home kept me in the news and there was no news about Beau Davis. He was presumed dead. By the time 1944 was coming to a close, and after all the death I had seen, I accepted that as fact. And then I met my Randolph, an officer and surgeon in the Medical Corp. We met bending over a soldier shot up and needing to be put back together again. There were many soldiers we worked on as a surgical team. We married simply in '46 when we returned home; this time home was Virginia."

Our tea was quite cold by then. Miss Sydney asked if she should ring for hot water. But I needed no more. Nor did she.

"We were so happy together back on American soil, adjusting to civilian life, happy when the babies began to come. We were happy with the first one, a boy in '47 the second, another boy in '49. Happy was the key word.

"Then the bomb dropped in 1950 by way of

this box coming to me in Virginia after first being re-routed
from my childhood home in Georgia. It was from Beau
Davis who was still in France. No one ever heard from him
since that last letter I received in1942 and the notice sent to
his mother that he was missing in action. The note tucked
in the box said:

My Dearest Sydney,
This is my gift to you to wear on our wedding night
which I'm looking forward to when I arrive home next
month. I've waited so long.
Love forever,
Your Beau Davis

Since the box took two weeks to find me, he would be
home in two weeks! I was pregnant with our third child, a
girl due in '51. I was appalled! Had I given up hope too
soon? Had I been disloyal? Unfaithful? Where did my
loyalties lie? How could I be so happy when he must have
been suffering somewhere.

Thankfully Randolph kept a cool head and a brain with
logical thinking. He knew of my youthful first love for
Beau Davis and broken heart before we met.

"Calm down." Randolph reasoned as he tucked me
into his protective arms. "Let's go into the kitchen and have
a cup of coffee and talk about this. Better yet, it's after 4
p.m. Let's have a pre-dinner glass of wine."

He brought out the fine crystal stemware and
poured, while I made a small tray of Gouda, Swiss, and
Tomme de Savoie cheeses with small slices of apple and

some French Baguette. The problem looked a little more manageable already.

Randolph said, "if Beau Davis was a prisoner of war or in a hospital, his family would have been notified. If he was detained for military purposes until now, five years after the war ended, how could he afford such an exquisite gift? This doesn't make sense. We just have to wait for his explanation. If you want me by your side when he comes, I'm here. If you want to meet him alone first, I understand."

Sydney smiled. I could tell she was seeing what I was hearing. "Since I'm here you know it worked out. When Beau Davis arrived in Georgia his mom filled him in on my marital status and that she approved; actually, liked my choice of husband. I always kept in touch with her. He certainly also owed me an explanation. He didn't come but he wrote:

Dear Sydney,
Mom has given me your full story. I wish you great
happiness. I was injured in Italy where a family took me in
and kept me safely hidden until the end of the war. I was
too unsettled to come home at that time. I have made a new,
successful life in Italy and expected to bring you back with
me. Forgive me for not contacting you sooner.
Be happy,
Beau Davis

"I could never wear this beautiful peignoir but just stuck it into the back of the closet and really forgot about it until it popped up when I readied to move here. It didn't seem right to toss it in the trash. It's too fine. So, after all this time it is still like new. I hope you will accept this little token to remember me by. It will feel lovely against your skin.

"Let me add one more thing," she said laughing heartily now, "Randolph gifted me a gorgeous French silk peignoir set, not in the ivory for a bride, but in sensuous black. My fourth child, another boy, was conceived the first night I wore it."

*Note: My dear friend, the late Anne Dippold Peterson did receive a gift of a beautiful ivory silk peignoir set from an elderly woman for which she was companion and caretaker. It was in a lovely Saks Fifth Avenue box with white tissue.

Anne asked me at the time to write a story about it, but the story never came to me until now, years after Anne has transitioned to the other side. I'm thinking she looked over my shoulder as I wrote this story. I could smell the Patchouli scent she favored. It was not the JOY that her lady liked.

Arlene S. Bice

About Our Authors

Nancy Lee Badger grew up on New York's Long Island. She swam at beaches on both the north and south shores. After marrying her college sweetheart and raising two sons in New Hampshire, Nancy moved to North Carolina. She's published in romance, a blogger, reviewer, and member of the Triangle Association of Freelancers.

Lois Thompson Bartholomew earned a BA in English from Brigham Young University and an MA in Publishing from Western Colorado University. A member of SCBWI and TAF, her YA novel The White Dove was published by Houghton Mifflin and republished by PennCreekPress. She is a lover of reading, writing, and books,

Arlene S. Bice is a writer of local history (NJ), poetry, metaphysics, memoir, fiction, and short stories. Her story is from her most recent book, Rumors and Other Short Stories. Her website is: arlenebice.com She lives in Farmville, Virginia.

Anne Glasser Brennan is an inspirational essayist, retreat leader and speaker from Cary, North Carolina. Her first book, God Does Not Take Naps, A Collection of Inspirational Essays, Poems and Reflections is readying for publication. Anne is a Pastoral Care Ministry volunteer and aspires to be a hospice chaplain.

Lauren Clemmons is a published author based in Raleigh, North Carolina. Her essays, poetry, and fiction appear in anthologies, including TAF publications.

Tom Harmon is an amateur writer living with his wife in Ontario, Canada. As an ex-pat from Florida, his writing is informed by his constantly changing scenery, both as a child and now as an adult. As a horror and science fiction writer, he uses the spectrum of human emotion and the uncertainty of new science to relate the lingering sense of dread all people have felt in new landscapes; both emotional and physical.

Marvis Henderson-Daye is a member of the Triangle Association of Freelancers. This is her fourth submission for TAF Anthologies. In addition, she published Nine Lives, Every Storm Runs Out of Rain, and a children's series, Grandmomma M. When she is not writing, she is dancing across the world.

Erika V. Hoffman taught high school, raised her four children, and now writes non-fiction narratives, travel articles, and educational pieces. Her books are collections of her published stories and personal essays.

Dorothy La Motta has published children's books, romance, fiction, non-fiction and poetry. Her work is featured in multiple anthologies, and the North Carolina Historical and Literary Journals. She holds membership in Triangle East Writers, Triangle Association of Freelancers, North Carolina Writers Network and Triangle East Chamber of Commerce.

Nanette Lavoie-Vaughan is an advanced practice nurse who has published clinical articles and book chapters and is the author of Healing Energy, Healing Hands, a guide to Therapeutic Touch. This is her first published short story.

Jesse McCorvey is a freelancer who has written numerous pieces throughout his career, mostly short stories and poems, and a few songs along the way. This is the beginning of his first novel about a widowed woman's strength, hardened by rebellion and unexpected life situations, and the spectacular legacy she creates.

Terri DeGezelle Michels is author and photographer, has published 64 children's non-fiction books, as well as more than 100 magazine articles, and a fiction picture book, Simon of Cyrene, Legend of the Easter Egg. Terri shares her art and writing experiences during school visits where she encourages students to follow their dreams.

K Ann Pennington is fascinated by the constructed nature of place in America. She focuses specifically on primary source materials and performing field research on a variety of topics, especially the Civil War. More about K Ann's stories can be found at:
https://kannpennington.wordpress.com/

Mike Rumble by day, works in Corporate America and by night morphs into a freelance writer with his own blog. He has published in Chicken Soup for the Soul: O Canada and assorted anthologies. Mike is also a Certified Professional

Resume Writer (CPRW) and writes articles for 5-West
magazine.

Sarah Merritt Ryan is a poet, blogger, and writer of
memoir. She writes of her experiences with emotionally
surviving serious mental illness, expressing her unique
story. Her poetry has been published by Whispering Angels
Books, Prolific Pulse Press, PurpleStone Press, Garden of
Neuro Institute, and Fine Lines Literary Journal.

Margaret Toman vigils in front of Central Prison every
Monday, advocating against the death penalty. Retired, she
is a former long-term caregiver who writes memoir, letters
to the editor, Op Eds and participates in discussion groups
about current affairs. She relishes classical music,
asparagus and mischievous Whiskey sours.

Lisa Tomey-Zonneveld is the founder/manager of Prolific
Pulse Press LLC and a widely published poet and writer.
She is an editor of numerous anthologies and for Fine Lines
Journal. She is Poet Laureate Emeritus of Garden of Neuro
Institute and is an organizer for Living Poetry in North
Carolina. ProlificPulse.blog

Don Vaughan is a freelance writer based in Raleigh, North
Carolina, and the founder of Triangle Association of
Freelancers.

Chanah Wizenberg received her BA from Hunter College
in English and Creative Writing. Her poetry and short
stories have appeared in several magazines and

anthologies. Chanah has been a professional ballerina, a pastry chef, and English teacher. She resides in Raleigh, North Carolina with her dog, Asha, and her cat, Marmalade.

About Our Editor

Arlene S. Bice is the author of more than a dozen non-fiction books on New Jersey history, memoir, metaphysics, short story fiction, and poetry. Her poems A Writer's Pandemic and New Orleans were performed in the Pandemic Blues at the Kirby Theatre directed by Fred Motley in Roxboro, (NC). She is the recipient of the Florence Poets Society Poet of Distinction Award, published in several anthologies, and is an award-winning artist. The Second Annual Oakley Hall Literary Award was presented to her in 2018.

She has consistently led writing groups since 1996. Pre-pandemic she hosted Poetry in Nature afternoons in the garden at Backyard Birds and the Rosemont Vineyard.

Ms Bice is former proprietor of By the Book @ U & I Gift Shop (NJ) for nearly 20 years and wrote a book review column for the Register-News for 10 years. World travel is a passion. She is an on-going student of past life regression and parapsychology.

Ms. Bice is a co-founding member of the Warren Artists Market (WAM) and holds memberships in Triangle Association of Freelancers (TAF), Nonfiction Authors Association (NFAA), and International Women's Writing Guild (IWWG). She holds Lifetime memberships in the Bordentown Historical Society (NJ) and New Egypt Historical Society (NJ)

She is an avid reader who lives in Virginia. Her latest book is Rumors and Other Short Stories. Her latest anthology is The Family Tree, an ancestor anthology.

Website: arlenebice.com

Acknowledgements

There are multiple hands, hearts, and minds that go into publishing a book and all deserve a nod of recognition. Thank you to every new TAF member for bravery in submitting their words for a first time publication. Thank you to each professional TAF member who takes time out of their working hours to contribute an unpaid submission for TAF's benefit.

To each of our speakers on TAF Talks and the guests at our meetings, who continue to share the secrets of their successes, to make the way a little easier for upcoming and ongoing writers. They permit us to create podcasts of interviews to share with our members. TAF Talks are a special perk of membership.

A huge amount of gratitude goes to John Wood for working his usual magic in creating YouTube links from our meetings

 To Maya for her introduction and Don for a brief history.

Always to Founder Don Vaughan who expands his influence with invitations and interviews with seasoned authors, artists, editors, playwrights, publicists, etc. He brings his many connections through years of freelance writing to benefit all TAF members. A huge Thank You.

A special Thank You to each reader who enjoyed our TAF Omnibus III and left a review on Amazon Books. It helps bring us into the public eye.

Membership

Membership in Triangle Association of Freelancers (TAF) provides:

Monthly meetings, presently virtual, with advance notice of guest speakers; often included are prominent authors, artists, editors, playwrights, publicists, etc.

Participation in TAF's "brain trust," which includes access to writing and publishing professionals with years (sometimes decades) of experience. Colleagues are eager to help you find success as a writer.

Publish in our annual omnibus and/or monthly blog.

Significantly discounted admission to the Write Now! Conference.

Access to writer resources in the members-only section of this site.

Ongoing support and encouragement for/from like-minded professionals.

Access to TAF's closed messaging forum, which is how members create writing friendships, share timely information and are open to job leads.

Inclusion in our Find A Freelancer professional profiles on our Website.

Membership in a generous, welcoming association that treats you like family. Won't you join us?

https://tafnc.com/member-benefits/

Books make great gifts because they have whole worlds inside of them.

Neil Gaiman